"I'm not about to give up, and neither are you. So why don't we work together?"

"What makes you think I want your help, Megan?" Garrett asked.

"You haven't caught Velasquez yet, have you? Maybe you need a fresh angle. The alternative is to keep wasting time dodging me."

She had a point. And he had to grudgingly admit the woman had style and ability. The fact that there was also this undercurrent of electricity running through him, this growing desire to find out just what the lady was truly made of, won him over.

"If I say yes, we play by my rules."

She laughed for the first time, and there was something about the sound that went right through him. "Partners? Don't worry, Wichita, I know exactly where I stand with you."

That, Garrett figured, put her one up on him.

Dear Reader,

It's summer, the perfect time to sit in the shade (or the air conditioning!) and read the latest from Silhouette Intimate Moments. Start off with Marie Ferrarella's newest CHILDFINDERS, INC. title, *A Forever Kind of Hero*. You'll find yourself turning pages at a furious rate, hoping Garrett Wichita and Megan Andreini will not only find the child they're searching for, but will also figure out how right they are for each other.

We've got more miniseries in store for you this month, too. Doreen Roberts offers the last of her RODEO MEN in *The Maverick's Bride*, a fitting conclusion to a wonderful trilogy. And don't miss the next of THE SISTERS WASKOWITZ, in Kathleen Creighton's fabulous *One Summer's Knight*. Don't forget, there's still one sister to go. Judith Duncan makes a welcome return with *Murphy's Child*, a FAMILIES ARE FOREVER title that will capture your emotions and your heart. Lindsay Longford, one of the most unique voices in romance today, is back with *No Surrender*, an EXPECTANTLY YOURS title. And finally, there's Maggie Price's *Most Wanted*, a MEN IN BLUE title that once again allows her to demonstrate her understanding of romance and relationships.

Six marvelous books to brighten your summer—don't miss a single one. And then come back next month, when six more of the most exciting romance novels around will be waiting for you—only in Silhouette Intimate Moments.

Enjoy!

Yours,

Leslie J. Wainger
Executive Senior Editor

Please address questions and book requests to:
Silhouette Reader Service
U.S.: 3010 Walden Ave., P.O. Box 1325, Buffalo, NY 14269
Canadian: P.O. Box 609, Fort Erie, Ont. L2A 5X3

MARIE FERRARELLA

A FOREVER KIND OF HERO

Published by Silhouette Books

America's Publisher of Contemporary Romance

To Alison Okazaki,
With fond thoughts,
From Jessica's mom

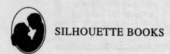 SILHOUETTE BOOKS

ISBN 0-373-07943-5

A FOREVER KIND OF HERO

This edition published by arrangement with Harlequin Books S.A.

® and TM are trademarks of Harlequin Books S.A., used under license.
Trademarks indicated with ® are registered in the United States Patent
and Trademark Office, the Canadian Trade Marks Office and in other
countries.

Visit us at www.romance.net

Printed in U.S.A.

Books by Marie Ferrarella

Silhouette Intimate Moments
*Holding Out for a Hero #496
*Heroes Great and Small #501
*Christmas Every Day #538
Callaghan's Way #601
*Caitlin's Guardian Angel #661
‡Happy New Year—Baby! #686
The Amnesiac Bride #787
Serena McKee's Back in Town #808
A Husband Waiting to Happen #842
Angus's Lost Lady #853
This Heart for Hire #919
††A Hero for all Seasons #932
††A Forever Kind of Hero #943

Silhouette Romance
The Gift #588
Five-Alarm Affair #613
Heart to Heart #632
Mother for Hire #686
Borrowed Baby #730
Her Special Angel #744
The Undoing of Justin Starbuck #766
Man Trouble #815
The Taming of the Teen #839
Father Goose #869
Babies on His Mind #920
The Right Man #932
In Her Own Backyard #947
Her Man Friday #959
Aunt Connie's Wedding #984
†Caution: Baby Ahead #1007
†Mother on the Wing #1026
†Baby Times Two #1037
Father in the Making #1078
The Women in Joe Sullivan's Life #1096
‡Do You Take This Child? #1145
The Man Who Would Be Daddy #1175
Your Baby or Mine? #1216
**The Baby Came C.O.D. #1264
Suddenly...Marriage! #1312
‡‡One Plus One Makes Marriage #1328
‡‡Never Too Late for Love #1351

Silhouette Desire
‡Husband: Optional #988

Silhouette Special Edition
It Happened One Night #597
A Girl's Best Friend #652
Blessing in Disguise #675
Someone To Talk To #703
World's Greatest Dad #767
Family Matters #832
She Got Her Man #843
Baby in the Middle #892
Husband: Some Assembly Required #931
Brooding Angel #963
‡Baby's First Christmas #997
Christmas Bride #1069
Wanted: Husband, Will Train #1132
Wife in the Mail #1217

Silhouette Yours Truly
‡The 7lb., 2oz. Valentine
Let's Get Mommy Married
Traci on the Spot
Mommy and the Policeman Next Door
**Desperately Seeking Twin...
The Offer She Couldn't Refuse
ΔFiona and the Sexy Stranger
ΔCowboys Are for Loving
ΔWill and the Headstrong Female
ΔThe Law and Ginny Marlow
ΔA Match for Morgan

Silhouette Books

In The Family Way

Silhouette Christmas Stories 1992
"The Night Santa Claus Returned"

Fortune's Children
Forgotten Honeymoon

World's Most Eligible Bachelors
Detective Dad

†Baby's Choice
‡The Baby of the Month Club
**Two Halves of a Whole
*Those Sinclairs
ΔThe Cutlers of the Shady Lady Ranch
‡‡Like Mother, Like Daughter
††ChildFinders, Inc.

Books by Marie Ferrarella writing as Marie Nicole

Silhouette Desire
Tried And True #112
Buyer Beware #142
Through Laughter And Tears #161
Grand Theft: Heart #182
A Woman of Integrity #197
Country Blue #224
Last Year's Hunk #274
Foxy Lady #315
Chocolate Dreams #346
No Laughing Matter #382

Silhouette Romance
Man Undercover #373
Please Stand By #394
Mine by Write #411
Getting Physical #440

MARIE FERRARELLA

lives in Southern California. She describes herself as the tired mother of two overenergetic children and the contented wife of one wonderful man. This RITA Award-winning author is thrilled to be following her dream of writing full-time.

Chapter 1

"Gotcha."

Garrett Wichita muttered the single word under his breath, a feeling of minor triumph flowing over him. The word was directed at the photograph of the young teenage girl he had just called up on the computer monitor.

Because he'd trained himself to double-check everything, even when he was certain, Garrett held up the ink-jet printout he'd made earlier, comparing it to the picture on the screen. The printout represented a single frame from literally miles of surveillance tape taken five nights ago at the Zanadu Casino in Las Vegas. It was a blowup of a girl walking beside a man wearing a white suit. What had struck Garrett originally was how young she looked. Too young to be there.

It was a shade less than a three-quarter profile, and calling it blurry was being charitable—but it was a match. He was almost positive.

Sometimes, "almost" had to do.

At least investigating the man's companion was something new to go on. Something that might help spring the trap faster, catch the quarry a little sooner.

Pressing the appropriate combination of keys, Garrett listened as the ink-jet printer on his desk came to life, printing the girl's photograph from the web site and the few lines of information that went with it. Her home was in a Southern California neighborhood, not too far from L.A.

Once he'd realized her age, Garrett had called up several internet sites that dealt exclusively with runaways and missing kids. She was one of a sea of countless faces. Garrett counted himself lucky that he'd found her after only a couple of hours, before he went cross-eyed—or worse, missed her because he'd become less discerning.

He leaned back, impatient for the printer to finish. Garrett drummed his fingers on his desk.

The site had been only the second one he'd pulled up. Sad how many sites like this there were these days, he thought. Sites devoted to kids who'd disappeared, thinking they could make a go of it in a world that they were ill-equipped to face.

He couldn't help wondering how many of those faces would have *deceased* stamped over their files before the year was out.

There but for the grace of God…

Hell, he thought, he *had* gone that route.

Except that he'd been one of the lucky ones. Lucky to have had the sense to pull himself out before he was found dead in some alley, before he had traded his soul for his next meal.

Before he'd gone down the route that his brother Andy had.

His mouth curved into a smile that had no feeling behind it—only memories.

It had been a little like old home week, scrolling through the endless parade of faces, most smiling as they posed for their picture before things had somehow gone sour in their young lives, for one reason or another. The faces had changed some from the ones he'd known. But not all that much. There was still hope there, in the eyes of some of them—hope for the future. The eyes he'd looked into when he was that age—and his own—had been dead.

Hopeless.

He wondered about the girl's eyes as the color reproduction inched its way out of the mouth of the printer. Was there still hope there? Or had she gotten sucked into a world she had no control over? A world that was most likely a hundred times worse than anything she'd found to rebel against at home.

Most likely, he thought again. But not always.

For a little while, the street had seemed like a blessing to him, too.

Garrett shut his memories away as the printer came to a whining halt, spitting out the end of the paper. Garrett picked up the photograph and examined it. The girl who looked up at him from the page was very pretty: blond, blue-eyed. She appeared to be a typical teenager—happy.

The likeness he'd seen on the tape hadn't been. Watching her, she'd reminded him of a puppet whose strings had been cut, but who hadn't realized it yet. She hadn't yet sank bonelessly to the floor. If it *was* the same girl, she'd lost weight. Too much weight.

Jorge Velasquez liked his runners thin, Garrett recalled. Velasquez had started out as a two-bit hustler, but through cunning, luck and a ruthless disregard for life, had managed to work his way up to the better sections of the southwest. Garrett had become aware of him before the transition had taken place.

"What are you up to, Kathy Teasdale?" he asked the photograph. "And what made you run away?"

"It was that boy, I know it." Judith Teasdale's voice hitched as she spoke. For a moment, she couldn't continue.

Looking helplessly at her guest—her last hope— Judith struggled to remain coherent, if not calm. Calm was something that had been cruelly wrenched from her grasp the morning she'd discovered the note on her teenage daughter's rumpled bed. The note that echoed Kathy's last words as she had stormed out of the house the previous night—"I'm out of here."

Warren Teasdale had dragged his daughter back that night, grounding her and sending her to her room. But neither Judith nor her husband had heard Kathy slip out sometime during the night. Slip out of the house and out of their lives.

After three weeks with no word from Kathy and no positive word from the police, Judith was terrified that the disappearance was permanent.

Her stomach tied in gargantuan knots, Judith turned toward the woman standing beside her—the woman she'd called when the police had told her that they were doing all they could to find Kathy and it hadn't been enough. The woman, Judith fervently prayed, who would hand her a miracle.

Judith drew in a huge breath, trying to sound more in control. "Ever since she met that boy, Joe Something-or-other, Kathy's been different. Defiant. I don't even know who she is anymore." Her eyes filled with tears, reddening again. "Or where she is."

Beginning to sob, she turned her face away, burying it against her husband's shoulder. Built like a linebacker, a position he'd played in college, Warren Teasdale closed his arm around his wife's shoulder. A silent appeal was in the eyes that he turned toward his guest.

Judith gave it sound. "Megan, please..."

"Megan, please, find him. Find your brother and bring him home." Even after two decades, Megan Andreini could still hear her mother saying those words. Time hadn't made the voice any softer, or made the acute stab of helplessness she had felt in response any duller.

But then she hadn't been able to fulfill the request. She'd only been eight at the time. Things were different now. She had experience and training, and this was her calling. She would find this missing child, just as she had found all those other missing children for the clients who came to ChildFinders, Inc. It was her destiny, her mission in life. And the only clear reason, Megan felt, that she was put on this earth: so that other people wouldn't suffer endlessly the way her mother had.

The way her brother had.

And the way she had.

Megan covered Judith's outstretched hand with her own. "Don't worry, we'll find her," she promised.

The promise was firm, unshakable. Megan knew firsthand just how much Kathy's parents needed to hear that. It was all they had to cling to: a promise from a woman they knew in passing through a mutual friend.

But at closer examination there was more to it. Megan knew what gave them solace was the fact that she was one-third of ChildFinders, Inc., an agency devoted to finding missing children throughout the country, founded by a man whose own son had been abducted. Cade Townsend's agency now had a sterling reputation and a perfect track record....

Except for one case. Its first one. But that was still open, ongoing. Megan had every faith in the world that one day, it too would be closed. Cade Townsend wasn't the kind who would ever accept defeat.

And neither was she.

Megan smiled kindly at Judith, who seemed to be drawing up her courage. "Thanksgiving is almost here. We've never been apart for the holidays. Kathy—'' Judith's voice broke.

Megan could feel her heart twisting. She knew what this felt like. She knew, too, what it was like to witness the pain without being able to say or do anything to help.

But Thanksgiving was only a few days away, and Megan was practical.

"Maybe I won't have her here in time for Thanksgiving—'' her voice was soft "—but I'll try to have her home before Christmas," she promised them.

"Warren, why don't you go get Judith a glass of water?'' she suggested politely. "And then you can answer some questions.''

"More questions?'' Warren asked impatiently as he crossed to the kitchen.

Megan heard him running the water. She made sure there was not a hint of doubt on her face as she looked at him when he returned. Doubt would only serve to stimulate their imagination and cause them further anguish. She was here to help alleviate that, not add to it.

"I'm going to need as much information about your daughter as you can give me.''

Judith pursed her lips and nodded. Warren pressed the glass of water into his wife's hand.

"Why don't you sit down and be more comfortable?'' Megan coaxed, indicating the sofa. She was accustomed to taking charge. She had been doing it for as long as she could remember.

An hour later, Megan's hand was beginning to

cramp as she wrote quickly, trying to keep up with
what Kathy's parents were telling her. Their voices
overlapped, each hurrying to answer her questions. As
if faster answers would bring Kathy back to them more
quickly.

The more she wrote, the more unlikely a candidate
Kathy Teasdale seemed to be for the role of a runaway.

Megan was surprised how much the Teasdales
seemed to know about their daughter's habits and her
friends. Most parents of teenagers Megan had dealt
with had a shadowy knowledge, at best, of their children's activities and the people who inhabited those
children's lives. The girl who was emerging from all
this information had been a bright, sunny, well-
adjusted fourteen-year-old who made the dean's list
every marking period.

Kathy seemed to be every mother's dream of a
daughter. What had turned the dream so sour? Was it
just sudden teenage angst, or was there more to it than
that?

She raised her eyes to the couple on the sofa, their
hands clasping in a united front against a world that
had taken their daughter from them.

As she asked her questions, Megan studied their
faces carefully, looking for any nonverbal indication
of darker secrets hidden in their family closet.

"No arguments, no hostility?"

Judith bit her lower lip and shook her head.

"None. Not until she started going out with this Joe
character," Warren said bitterly. He looked at Judith,

a helplessness entering his eyes. "I told you she was too young to start seeing boys."

"I know," Judith whispered. "You were right. But she begged so—"

Megan wedged her question in before the discussion could break down into accusations. She'd witnessed it happening before. "Do you know if he's missing, too?"

Warren and Judith looked at one another before turning toward Megan and shaking their heads in unison. Joe What's-his-name was a person completely outside their realm. It was obvious that it had never even occurred to either of them to find the teenager and question him.

"We have no idea," Warren told her.

Megan saw how tightly Warren was holding onto his wife's hand throughout the questioning. They were drawing strength from one another. To the outside observer, they seemed like the perfect family.

A perfect family, Megan thought, that was shattering.

She had nothing but empathy for them. Her own family had shattered a long time ago. Just how fully, she hadn't realized until several years later, during the first of her mother's stays at the hospital.

Megan looked down at her notes, counting on memory to help her decipher them later. Her handwriting was every bit as awful as Sam Walters, her other partner, said it was. Maybe worse.

She flipped to the next empty page. "I'm going to

need a last name for this Joe.'' Megan looked from
one parent to the other, waiting.

But they had no answer for her.

A light came into Judith's eyes. "Sharon would
know." She turned to Megan. "Sharon is Kathy's best
friend."

Megan had already noted Sharon's last name and
her telephone number. She planned to talk to the girl,
as well as to several of the other teenagers that the
Teasdales had mentioned.

But there might be a quicker way to find out the
last name of this Joe, who had taken a perfectly lovely
suburban girl and hypnotically transformed her into
every parent's nightmare. Megan rose to her feet.
"May I see her room?"

"Yes, of course." Indicating to her husband to remain where he was, Judith rose from the sofa and led
the way to the stairs.

Megan noted that her gait appeared much heavier
than that of a trim woman of thirty-eight. It was as if
she'd aged twenty years in the last twenty days: one
year for each day her daughter had been missing from
her life. Megan thought of her own mother and the
two-and-a-half year vigil that Margaret Andreini had
kept, waiting for Chad to be returned.

No one should have to go through anything like
that.

Stopping at the second room to the right of the
stairs, Judith opened the door. She stood there, at the
threshold, peering in, as if willing her daughter to appear.

"I haven't touched anything," Judith said softly.

Megan lightly touched Judith's shoulder as she passed. She understood, recalling her own mother's words.

I'm keeping your brother's room just the way he left it. So when he comes home, he won't be upset.

Entering, she looked around slowly. It was a typical room that might have belonged to any upper middle-class fourteen-year-old, maybe a little neater than most. Megan remembered that when she was Kathy's age her own room had always looked like a hurricane had passed through.

There were posters taped to the walls. Current heart-throbs of the puppy-love set, she mused. No clothes on the floor.

Maybe the girl wasn't all that typical, Megan decided. She looked over her shoulder at Judith. "I need to poke around."

Judith's head bobbed up and down. "Anything. Anything that might help," she whispered.

The doorbell chimed, and Judith looked flustered at the intrusive noise. Indecision washed over her thin, pale features.

"I think someone's at your front door. Why don't you go and answer it?" Megan coaxed tactfully.

It was just as well. She did better without someone looking over her shoulder.

A flicker of light entered the other woman's eyes. "Maybe there's news."

Clutching to hope as if it were a talisman, Judith

Teasdale turned and flew down the stairs to see who was ringing her doorbell.

Megan wasted no time.

Quickly, efficiently, she opened closets, riffled through drawers, turned up the mattress. She touched on all the places that a young girl would use to hide things from her parents and discovered, amazingly enough, that Kathy seemed to have no secrets. There were no drugs of any type, no condoms or contraceptives. Not even a racy video or forbidden magazine.

For all intents and purposes, Kathy seemed squeaky clean and as straight as an arrow.

Except that she was a runaway.

It looked as if Joe What's-his-name was Megan's strongest lead. The power of first love was overwhelming, Megan mused.

The only thing that Megan found, after her search of the small, stuffed-animal-filled room, was a diary. It was the garden-variety type, obtained at any stationery store or card shop. It came complete with a gleaming, gold-plated lock. The key was nowhere to be seen.

But that wasn't an obstacle. Megan worked open the lock with minimal effort. "Sorry, Kathy," she apologized to the absent teenager as she flipped through to the end of the book, looking for the place where Kathy had left off, "but this is for your own good."

Voices from the first floor floated up to Megan. She heard a deep masculine one, as well as the Teasdales speaking. Megan couldn't make out the words as she read through the last entry, but the tone registered nonetheless, piquing her interest. The man had a deep, authoritative voice. It was the kind of voice that belonged to someone who naturally took charge of things. As she walked to the head of the stairs, she continued to scan the diary.

The portrait of a very young girl, naively in love for the first time and willing to do anything for a teenage boy she considered exciting and dangerous, began taking form.

A teenage boy called Joe Stafford.

She had a name.

Pleased, Megan shoved the diary into her shoulder bag on top of the notes she'd taken. It was a good start. Hopefully, it would be good enough.

That settled, curiosity came at her from a different direction. Wondering why Judith hadn't returned to Kathy's bedroom, Megan made her way down the stairs. The voices were clearer now.

Intrigued, Megan stood quietly in the doorway, intent on observing the man sitting in the Teasdales' living room.

Her first impression was that the dark-haired man with his back to her was in some branch of law enforcement. She was well acquainted with the breed, having worked with the FBI before finally throwing her lot in with Cade.

She could smell a cop—any sort of cop—a mile away. She thought she smelled one now.

There was something in the set of the man's shoulders, in the way he held himself, that gave him away.

She doubted that he was a policeman. He wasn't in uniform, so at the very least he would have to be a detective. But somehow, she didn't think so.

She knew most of the detectives in the area. This one didn't sound familiar. She caught a glimpse of his profile, and it confirmed her suspicions. She didn't know him. He appeared tall, even sitting down, and had the kind of rugged profile that would send a sculptor running for his chisel.

If he wasn't in law enforcement, he should be, she mused. He had an air about him that took center stage, the kind of bearing that made people sit up and listen even if they were disinclined to.

Megan crossed her arms before her, content to listen for a moment. She wondered how this man figured into the Teasdales' lives, and whether he was bringing them bad news.

Garrett sensed her presence even before he glanced toward the doorway. He'd gotten that back-of-the-neck-itchy-feeling maybe a second before he judged she'd made her appearance. He wasn't sure just why.

From the look of the petite, slim blonde, he would have guessed that she was Kathy's sister. Probably older, but if so, not by all that many years. And while the face of the girl, both in the photograph he held and in the framed one on the mantelpiece, was definitely clean scrubbed and sedate, one glance at the blonde in the doorway told him that she was probably a handful, by any definition.

There was a feistiness about the girl that telegraphed itself to him across the room. If he had been asked to pick which of the two sisters was the most likely to run away, Garrett would have picked her, rather than Kathy. She looked as if she could handle whatever was dished out with a great deal more ease.

Garrett had learned to be a quick judge of people and situations a long time ago. When you lived on the streets, you were either a quick judge, or a victim. And he allowed himself to be a victim only once. Never again.

Seeing Megan standing in the doorway, Warren motioned her into the room, rising from his seat. "Megan, this is Garrett Wichita. He's with the DEA."

"He thinks that he might have seen Kathy," Judith added excitedly.

Following Warren's example, Garrett rose to his feet as Megan approached. Watching her, he judged that he was about a foot taller than she was. Her size made him feel larger than he was.

The smile curving her mouth told him that she was aware of that.

Politely, he extended his hand to her. "Ms. Teasdale."

Judith looked confused for a moment, then recovered, shaking her head. She set the agent straight. "Oh no, Mr. Wichita, she's not related to us. This is Megan Andreini."

Judith said the name as if it was supposed to mean something to him. It didn't. Curious, Garrett raised an eyebrow. "A neighbor?" he guessed.

More than likely, Megan was one of Kathy's friends. So much the better. In his experience, the friends of a runaway usually knew considerably more than the parents did.

"A private investigator," Megan corrected. "The Teasdales have hired me to find their daughter." She smiled at him.

His eyes narrowed. He was rarely guilty of misjudging, but it was obvious that he had this time. Big time. But even if she wasn't Kathy's sister, she certainly didn't look old enough to have a detective's license. Someone had to be pulling his leg.

"Exactly how old are you?" The question came with no apology.

"Old enough." Megan was purposely evasive. "Obviously a lot older than you think I am. Didn't anyone ever tell you that it wasn't nice to ask a woman her age?"

It was one of her assets, looking far younger than her actual age. It gave her the ability to blend in with crowds of young people. She'd done some undercover work, posing as a high school student, but that had been while she was with the Bureau.

Still, at twenty-nine she knew she could still pass for eighteen if she had to. But it did at times get in the way of having people take her seriously. She could see it happening again with this DEA agent.

"Are you going to make my job easier?" She paused, looking into his eyes. "Or harder?"

Chapter 2

The last thing Garrett would have pegged the petite blonde with the heart-shaped face for was a private investigator.

Garrett weighed his options before giving his answer to the question Megan had put to him. This operation had lasted too long and cost too many lives. His main concern was trapping Jorge Velasquez and stopping the flow of cocaine and heroine into the upper-crust locations the man dealt with. Granted, Velasquez represented only one head of the Hydra, but for Garrett there was more at stake than just bringing down an established, large-scale drug dealer. Much more.

Tracking down Kathy Teasdale was just a means to a far greater end. A shaky means at that. By the time he found her—*if* he found her—Kathy might no longer have any contact with Velasquez or anyone in his far-reaching organization.

But to these people whose home he'd just entered, finding Kathy wasn't a means to an end. It was everything. He knew that.

He knew, too, that they were hoping for the teenager to return to them just the way she'd left—as bright-eyed, sweet-smiling and innocent as the girl in the photograph. They had no idea how impossible that was. They probably had no idea just what was out there.

You have to live it in order to understand it. And maybe not even then, he thought.

The girl they would get back—if she ever returned at all—would be a different person from the girl who had run away.

Garrett had the distinct impression that the woman who was making him squirm internally knew that.

"You still haven't answered my question, Mr. Wichita," Megan said, interrupting his thoughts.

"Actually, I was hoping that you—" he shifted his eyes toward Kathy's parents, for the moment ignoring Megan "—could do that for me." Both parents looked at him blankly. "Give me a clue as to where she was," he explained. "Have you heard from her?" He gazed at them intently, looking for signs of evasiveness, for lies that were badly covered. "Has she made any effort at all to contact either one of you in the last three weeks?"

"No." Accompanied by a strangled sob, the single word came from Judith.

"I wouldn't be asking for your help finding her, Mr. Wichita, if Kathy had called her parents," Megan pointed out mildly.

She congratulated herself on keeping her temper under control. Couldn't this big lug who was way overdue for a haircut see that? Why was he poking questions at these people when they were obviously both hurting so badly? With little effort, she remembered the police detectives who had come to question and re-question her mother after Chad had been kidnapped. They'd all but come out and accused her of killing her own son and then doing away with his body. It was that kind of treatment that had begun to send her mother over the brink.

Megan clenched her hands at her sides.

Warren squared his shoulders as he covered his wife's clasped hands again.

"What has she done?" His voice shook as he struggled for strength in the face of this newest turn. "I mean, why the DEA? Why are you here? Is Kathy in some kind of trouble?"

"She's—"

Garrett didn't know exactly what made him glance at the pint-size private investigator before answering Warren's question. Maybe it was instinct. Maybe it was because she was staring at him so hard that he could feel her eyes boring into his skull.

But whatever it was, when he did, he saw the warning look in her eyes. She was being protective of these people, letting him know that they were both in a fragile state and had to be treated accordingly.

He didn't particularly like being dictated to, even silently.

Garrett noted Megan's clenched hands before continuing. What was that about?

"No." As he spoke, he mentally amended his words. "She's not in any trouble. It's only that one of our surveillance tapes picked her up in the same area as a man we're looking to question." He showed them the photograph he'd had freeze-framed and printed. "We thought she might be able to tell us where he is." It was ground in the truth, but he knew it sounded flimsy.

Judith looked at the photograph, and a little gasp punctuated the bolt of recognition that shot through her. The girl in the picture was wearing a dress that was years too old for a fourteen-year-old.

Her hand was shaking as she handed the photograph back to Garrett. "What kind of man?"

Garrett heard the protective tone in Judith's voice. Protective and anguished at the same time, because there was nothing she could do for Kathy.

He left the photograph on the coffee table for now. There was no way to say this—except straight out. "His name is Jorge Velasquez and he's suspected of—"

"He has some information the DEA is trying to pin down," Megan interjected. She deliberately avoided looking in his direction. "Velasquez was in the witness protection program, but the system lost track of him."

"Witness protection program?" Warren echoed, appearing confused. "Is he dangerous?" he demanded, taking hold of Garrett's arm. "Is my daughter in any danger?"

Yes, Megan thought. *Your daughter's in a lot of danger.*

But it would do the Teasdales no good to know that—not when they had no way to get in contact with her, no way to help. They didn't need to have this additional cross to bear.

"Velasquez travels in completely different circles from a girl like Kathy," Megan assured them, her voice soft, comforting. She looked up at Garrett, warning him not to contradict her in front of the girl's parents. "I'm sure it's only a matter of her being in the same vicinity as Velasquez. Mr. Wichita is probably trying to find out if she might have overheard something that was being said." Her expression was pure sweetness as she faced him again with the Teasdales looking on. "Isn't that so, Mr. Wichita?"

Garrett felt as if her green eyes were digging into him with tiny, sharp points. There was no need for overkill; he got the message. Not that he cared for it much. He'd been right about her. The woman was trouble with a capital *T.*

And how does she know Velasquez and his reputation? he wondered.

"Yes, that's so," he agreed. "Then you really haven't heard anything at all from her? Not even an aborted communication?"

The tears that welled up in Judith's eyes answered his question for him. His sympathies were with them, but that couldn't be allowed to get in the way of this operation. He had to cover all bets.

He turned to Warren. "Would you mind if we put a tap on your telephone—in case she does try to contact you?"

Looking lost, bewildered, the couple held hands and glanced at Megan for guidance. Neither saw the slight frown that rose to Wichita's lips.

But Megan did. Apparently the man didn't care for being in the back seat.

Megan thought quickly. She was about to suggest the same thing, only using the agency's equipment. She would have preferred it that way. But if she told the Teasdales to refuse Wichita, clearing the way for her tap, that would run her absolutely afoul of the man. And she couldn't afford that. She wanted to stay on his good side. If the DEA agent was looking for Velasquez, and Kathy was somehow involved, chances were good that she could locate the girl if she kept Wichita in her sight.

He wouldn't cooperate if she stepped on his toes.

"It might be a good idea," Megan counseled the couple. They exchanged looks, still uncertain. "That way, if the DEA can get a lock on the call, we can use that to pinpoint Kathy's location. I can be there," she promised them firmly, "wherever it is, as fast as a car or plane can take me."

"All right." Warren nodded. "Do whatever you have to do." But his words seemed directed to Megan.

Garrett found it very irritating, having to operate through a go-between, especially someone who wasn't one of his operatives. But he banked down the feeling. He didn't have time to deal with unproductive emotions.

This far along in the operation, he didn't need or have the time for any emotions at all. He needed to remain sharp and alert.

And to stay alive.

"Fine, then we'll—"

"Where was Velasquez last seen?" Megan interrupted again.

Though Garrett gave no indication, she was quickly getting on his nerves.

"According to our records, it was the Beacon Hill region in San Francisco." What was she up to? he wondered. Not for a minute was he being taken in by the innocent expression on her face.

"May I see the photograph again?"

He took it out and handed it to her.

He'd brought this, Megan figured, to convince the Teasdales that he was on the level, in case they had their doubts. He had no way of knowing that the Teasdales were completely open, completely ready to believe anything they were told, as long as it meant that their daughter would be coming home to them.

Taking the photograph, she studied it. There was no mistaking what was in the background. Gambling was illegal in San Francisco. She raised her eyes to Garrett's. "Those are slot machines."

He had half a mind to ignore her, but it was through her that he remained on the Teasdales' good side. He had to keep all the options open until one of the

DEA's informants came through with a positive location for Velasquez's next exchange. That was when the net was finally going to drop on the dealer.

But right now, the target was out there somewhere, and he had to find him.

Garrett inclined his head. "The surveillance tape was from a Vegas casino."

Judith didn't understand. She laid a thin hand on Garrett's arm. "Is Kathy in Las Vegas?"

"She might be," Garrett allowed guardedly.

Although by now chances of the girl still being there were slim to none. Velasquez moved around a great deal. Again Garrett felt the blonde looking at him. Looking at him as if she knew what he'd just said wasn't true.

Garrett relented a little. "The tape is five days old."

Ten minutes later, he rose to his feet. There was nothing more for him here, for the time being. He now had a list of Kathy's friends, and permission to put in a tap. The Teasdales appeared to be honest, open people. The blonde's point was well taken. If they'd heard from their daughter, then they wouldn't have a private investigator in their living room, guarding their feelings like a junkyard dog.

A hell of an attractive junkyard dog, he allowed as his eyes critically swept over her again, but one he didn't particularly want to tangle with. There wasn't time for that.

Garrett made a mental note to find out what he could about Megan Andreini. He didn't like unknown elements posing a threat to his operation. He had been tracking down and hacking off Velasquez's tentacles, one by one, for a long time now. Soon he might have a chance to strike at the man himself. If his luck held.

All he wanted was the chance to bring Velasquez down. Permanently.

Opening his jacket, he took out a card. He held it out to Judith.

"This is my cell phone number, Mrs. Teasdale." Garrett looked from one of Kathy's parents to the other. They were nice people—two more lives that Velasquez had inadvertently touched and poisoned. "If you need me, call."

Judith accepted the card, just as Megan held out her hand to him. Puzzled, Garrett looked at her and raised a brow.

"I'd like one, too," Megan told him. "In case I need you."

Oh yeah, she was trouble all right. What really worried him was that he didn't know what kind. As for needing him—that was a crock. He had a strong hunch that she thought she could find her own way around easily enough.

Playing along, Garrett took out another card and handed it to her.

Megan glanced down at the white card, with its small, black lettering. The cell phone had an area code that wasn't local. For a second, she couldn't place it. And then it came to her. Texas.

Megan tucked the card into her breast pocket. "Where are you staying?"

He followed the movement of her hand, then realized that he was staring, and that she knew it. Garrett raised his eyes to her face.

"At the Random Hotel. I'll be gone by morning," he added.

He had other leads to work on, although right now, this was the strongest one. From the small amount he'd seen on the videotape, it looked as if Kathy had somehow landed, however unwittingly, in Velasquez's organization. She was just the kind of young, naive and easily manipulated teenager that the man had a penchant for using, and she had all the right qualifications.

She was underage and disposable.

Megan nodded in response to the hotel name, folding her fingers around the card. She was acquainted with the hotel. It was one of several that had sprouted up along MacArthur Boulevard, less than a stone's throw from John Wayne Airport.

Obviously, Wichita didn't like to waste time. She could admire that.

"I'll keep that in mind," she told him.

He wondered what she had up her sleeve, besides a rather well-toned arm. The condition of her arm indicated that she was serious about keeping in shape— and succeeding. That took discipline. He'd always admired discipline in people. Maybe it was because he knew how hard it was to maintain.

As a rule, he'd always found private investigators to be a royal pain, and he had a strong gut feeling that this one was no exception. But there was a possibility that there might be one interesting night in this for them. It had been a long time since he'd enjoyed the company of a woman, beautiful or otherwise, and this one, no matter how long a nose she was poking into his business, was certainly beautiful. The more he looked at her, the more he realized that.

The thought of spending the night with her was not without its appeal.

Time to go, he told himself. His thoughts were taking far too personal a bent.

"I'll be in touch," he told the Teasdales before turning on his heel.

"Should we be expecting someone?" Warren asked Garrett as he led the way to his front door. Like a wan shadow, Judith trailed behind them. "To see to the telephone," he added, when Garrett made no response.

"No, we can handle everything on our end," Garrett assured him. An external tap would prove simpler in this case. "I just wanted your permission."

The admission impressed Megan. Maybe Wichita wasn't such a bad guy, after all, she decided. For a government agent.

She knew that he could easily have just gone ahead with the tap without informing the Teasdales. It was one of those flexible, gray areas that didn't have to come up in court if an arrest actually materialized out of all this.

And the fact that Wichita hadn't contradicted her earlier explanation to the Teasdales told her that the man had some principles beyond his dedication to his job. That could prove useful to her down the line if she was actually forced to work with him.

"Thank you for your time," Garrett was saying to the couple at the front door.

Giving Megan a marginal nod, he turned away and walked to his car. He wanted to be away from the sadness hovering here. He'd already had his fill of sadness—enough to last two lifetimes.

It was one of the reasons—no, he amended, *the* main reason he was after scum like Velasquez. Because of the sadness.

And because of Andy.

Behind him, Megan was taking her leave of the Teasdales as well. "I'll be in touch."

Reaching his car, Garrett turned around just as she said it. He couldn't shake the feeling that somehow she was also putting him on notice as well.

He wondered if he was going to regret telling her of his whereabouts in the long run. But he shrugged the thought away as he got into his car. She was only a local private investigator, and he'd be gone by morning. How much of a problem could she be?

The petite blonde was almost out of his thoughts by the time he started the engine and pulled away from the curb.

Almost.

Hot, tired and disgusted, one hand holding the telephone receiver to his ear, Garrett loosened his tie, then yanked it off entirely. He discarded the offending appendage as he sank down on the hotel bed. It had been one of those endless, fruitless days when he felt like a dog chasing his own tail. *After a while, you almost forget why you're doing it,* he thought.

Looking back, he realized that talking to the Teasdales had been the definite high point of his day.

He scrubbed one hand over his face as he listened to his partner's voice on the other end of the line. Garrett didn't like what he was hearing about how the operation was proceeding in Texas, where Velasquez's main base of operation had begun.

Sighing, he began unbuttoning his shirt. "Give that to me again, Oscar."

"How many ways do you want me to tell you?" Frustration laced Oscar Juarez's voice. "It's been no picnic around here, you know. At least you're out there in California, away from the cold." The man on the other end paused before continuing. "We found an unidentified girl in an alley not too far away from Velasquez's last known base of operation. There were track marks on both arms. Coroner said she's been dead for over a week. The last snowstorm we're just digging out of must have slowed down the decomposition." His voice became muffled.

"Are you eating?"

"Hey, I've been going since six a.m. on those breakfast things. You know the ones I'm talking about. Two to a package. Wouldn't satisfy a squirrel. Wife's got me on a diet," he grumbled.

But Garrett wasn't interested in Oscar's diet, or what he was consuming at the moment. His mind had focused on the dead girl. He didn't like where this conversation was going.

"Coroner sure about the time of death?"

"Yeah, why?"

Garrett thought of Kathy's parents. "It's not the girl in the surveillance tape, is it? The runaway I found on the internet yesterday?" He'd shown the copy to his partner before coming out here.

"No way. Yours is a blonde, this one's a definite brunette. Or was. Looks older, too. Closer to eighteen. Hard to tell, really," he confessed. "Seems a damn shame. Why don't these kids stay at home?"

Garrett closed his eyes for a minute. Home had meant something to him—once. When there was still someone there for him. But after his parents and Andy had died, it became just another four-letter word littering his life.

"A hundred different reasons, Oscar. None of them amounting to a hill of beans when you weigh it against the alternative that girl in the alley met up with. I'm checking out in the morning. I'll call you if there's anything new to report."

He hung up as Oscar was mumbling a muffled "Goodbye" in his ear.

Replacing the receiver, Garrett sat on the edge of the bed, staring at the telephone. At least the Teasdales wouldn't be getting a phone call to come down and identify their daughter's body.

But eventually, another set of parents would.

The thought rankled him. By all rights, the net should have closed around Velasquez months ago. How many days was that when counted in lost lives?

Velasquez's runners were expendable, and there seemed to be an endless supply of them.

Just as there was an endless supply of his clients. Unsuspecting, bored rich teenagers looking for a "buzz," a shortcut to boundless happiness and thrills that didn't involve work, effort or any sort of disappointment. Or so they thought. They were all destined to be nameless, faceless statistics in some report.

And an ache in someone's heart.

Garrett laced his hands behind his head and stared grimly at the ceiling. Maybe he'd been at this too long. Maybe he'd lost his edge. Maybe someone fresher, newer would do a better job.

Annoyance washed over him. Maybe he'd better stop feeling, and start thinking again.

"I'll get you, you scum," he swore quietly under his breath. "There isn't a rock large enough for you to crawl under and hide. No lawyer clever enough to keep saving your worthless skin. Someday, some way, I'll get the goods on you, Velasquez, and then you'll rot," he promised himself.

And Andy.

The phone rang, and his body tensed immediately.

Had Oscar forgotten to tell him something? Garrett wasn't entirely sure if he wanted to hear anything else tonight. Maybe he was too tired, but part of him just wanted to forget for a little while. Lately he'd been feeling as if he were running on empty.

Garrett reached for the receiver and brought it to his ear. "Hello?"

"Wichita?" The sexy, low voice immediately filled

his ear and stirred him. It was a striking contrast to Oscar's muffled tenor. "This is Megan Andreini. I'm in the lobby."

"I'll be right down."

Holding up his wrist, Garrett looked at his watch. She was earlier than he thought she'd be. Sitting up, he began rebuttoning his shirt. His exhaustion drained miraculously away.

Chapter 3

The first thing that occurred to Garrett when he walked out of the elevator and into the lobby was that he must have been blind earlier. Only a blind man could have actually thought that Megan Andreini looked like anybody's kid sister. The blonde in the form-fitting turquoise dress standing near the front desk might have been someone's sister, all right, but she was also definitely all woman.

By the look in the desk clerk's eyes, the man thought the same. The package might be small, Garrett mused, approaching, but it was sexy as hell.

What she had on was a far cry from the simple jeans and loose pullover sweater she'd had on earlier. The lady was dressed to kill. Garrett had more than a strong hunch he knew just who the prey was.

Knowing didn't stop him from entering the game.

He lengthened his stride, crossing to Megan before someone else had an opportunity to engage her in conversation. The look he gave her as he greeted her was long on appreciation. Garrett figured she deserved her due.

"You clean up rather nicely."

From the corner of her eye, Megan had watched him get off the elevator and cross to her. She turned toward him now, knowing what she was doing was obvious and hoping to trap him in his own overconfidence. She'd learned that most people relax when they think they've sized you up.

She wanted him relaxed. It was a lot easier getting information that way.

Wichita looked tired, she thought. The slightly rumpled appearance just added to the appeal she suspected he was well aware of possessing. There was nothing bland or carbon-copy-like about this government agent. He stood out on his own—the kind of man who made women's heads turn, and men envious.

Megan smiled at Garrett as he joined her. "I had no idea I was that messy earlier."

So it was going to be like that, was it? Garrett thought. They were going to banter. Why not? He could use some mental diversion right about now. His mind was crowded with too many grim facts, too many daunting statistics. A little recreation was long overdue. As long as he didn't slip and forget himself in her company.

He couldn't help wondering how many men had already been guilty of that.

''Not messy, just a lot younger looking. You looked as if you were sixteen before.'' With a shrug, he dismissed his error. ''Must have been the light.''

The light, he observed, was just fine now, and incredibly friendly to her. She had flawless skin, highlighted by a minimum of makeup. Rather than appear fresh scrubbed, however, she looked quite capable of making a man swallow his own tongue in heated anticipation.

Megan casually lifted a shoulder, then let it drop, aware that he was watching her every movement. Out to captivate him, she was still flattered by the look in his eyes.

He made her feel warm. The man, she decided, was nothing short of smooth.

''People see what they expect to see. You were expecting Kathy's family. I fell into the category of sister.'' Her smile widened a little as she tilted her head up to his. ''Besides, people tell me I have a deceptively young face.''

Her face might be deceptively young, he thought, but her body certainly wasn't. From the way the clingy fabric was making love to it with every breath she took, he could see that her body was hard and firm and curved in places that made a man's mouth water and his imagination take flight.

Even a supposedly tired man.

Garrett smiled to himself. ''You do, actually.''

Megan found the smile that curved his mouth sexy and tinged with amusement. And—if she gave it any thought—arousing.

His smile widened. "'Fraid I wasn't looking at your face just now."

"I noticed." For a second, held fast by the look in his eyes, Megan had to remind herself who was the predator and who was the prey.

Her strategy was working. She'd come carefully groomed by design, not by accident.

After walking around the halls of Bedford High School for several hours, talking to Kathy's friends, Megan would much rather have been sitting shoeless, eating dinner in front of her television set. Instead, she'd donned her highest pair of heels and put on a dress that was guaranteed to make every man within a three-mile radius sit up and take notice. She would have hated to think all the preparation had been for naught.

The look in his eyes told her it hadn't.

Part of her felt as if she were playing dress-up. But men like Wichita weren't easily distracted, and tended to guard whatever pieces of information they had rather zealously. She wanted that information, needed whatever pieces of the puzzle she could get her hands on so she could try to make sense of things.

From what she could gather out of the fragments of information she'd gotten from Kathy's friends and a local youth coordinator, Joe Stafford hadn't been heard from since Kathy had disappeared. But unlike Kathy's situation, there was no one to care if Joe was missing or not.

His parents were divorced, remarried and living out of the state. Until recently, Joe had been staying with an older brother who had his hands full with his own unstable life. Nobody seemed to know where Joe was. Nobody cared. Megan found herself feeling sorry for the teenager.

She figured Kathy and Joe had gone off together; the straight-A student would never have had the courage to run away on her own. Plus, without him at her side, there would have been no reason to go anywhere.

So here she was, after putting in her full day, trying to charm whatever information she could out of a guy who looked less like a government agent than he did a woman's ideal fantasy man.

Some other woman's, but not hers. Megan knew that under that chiseled exterior beat a heart that was solid rock. She'd dealt with enough Garrett Wichitas in her time to have learned that.

Garrett no longer felt nearly as tired as he had upstairs in his hotel room. In fact, he was curious to know what Megan was after, and raring to go.

She had to be after something, he reasoned, dressed like that. He didn't flatter himself to think that she was after him alone.

"Why don't we go into the hotel restaurant?" He indicated the entrance to the right. The lighting became dimmer just beyond the opened threshold. He supposed that by some standards, it might even prove to be a romantic location. That might go along with whatever it was she thought she was planning, Garrett mused. After the day he'd put in, he could use a little entertaining. "I hear the food is rather good."

She wasn't really hungry, but that wasn't the point

of being here. Megan fixed an inviting smile on her face. "Sounds promising." She let him slip his arm around her shoulders to guide her inside. The contact was oddly electric, if she thought about it. So she didn't. Electricity also wasn't the point of being here.

"Have you had any time to eat yet?"

Her question surprised him. It was personal—the kind of question he would have anticipated from someone's mother, not a woman who looked as if she was out to charm the pants off him and con whatever she could out of him in the process.

On second thought, he supposed she said it to put him at ease.

"No, not yet." He caught the hostess's eye and nodded. The woman approached them. "Eating wasn't high on my priority list today."

Megan turned slowly, purposely brushing ever so slightly against him. The tingle that zipped through her was unanticipated—and momentarily distracting. It was a beat or two before she was focused again. "What was? Catching the bad guys?"

Garrett couldn't tell if she was actually mocking him, or still playing the game. Probably the latter. "Something like that."

After showing them to their table located in a raised portion of the restaurant and overlooking tables closer to the entrance, the hostess silently withdrew, leaving menus in her wake.

Garrett became vaguely aware that he was hungry, but his nascent appetite had nothing to do with food. He watched Megan as she slid into her seat across from him. His glance was slow and precise as it swept over her again. And doubly appreciative.

If she hadn't known that it wasn't possible, Megan would have said that she could *feel* his eyes slowly moving along her body.

It made her smile again.

"So—" Garrett opened the menu, but continued looking at her "—to what do I owe this visit?"

Following his example, she opened her menu and pretended to peruse it. "I thought maybe we could pool our information."

Like hell she did, he thought. "Or you could ferret out mine."

Megan raised her eyes from the menu, intrigued at what was behind his smile.

"I'm sure a smart man like you wouldn't allow that to happen." Pausing, she lowered her eyes again. "Unless he wanted it to."

The smile on her lips teased one out of the corners of his own mouth. The lady was something else, all right. She probably thought of herself as a femme fatale. It would have been easier to laugh off if she wasn't so damn attractive in that dress.

"And what—" he lowered his voice "—are you prepared to do, for me to want it to be?"

She closed the menu and held it against her, her attention riveted to him as if he was the most fascinating man in the world. A lesser man, Garrett told himself, would easily have bought into this.

"I could trade for it," she told him.

It was a good thing he knew that she was trying to

reel him in, or it might have actually happened, Garrett realized.

"What sort of trade?" Even as he asked, he could envision her in his bed, slowly peeling that dress away from every tempting swell. His mouth had become very dry. It took effort not to reach for the water glass.

"A name."

Garrett blinked. He hadn't expected that. Maybe it was the hour, although he was more inclined to think that it was the woman, that made him wish that she had something far more intimate in mind by way of a trade. Embraces and hastily mumbled, quickly forgotten words in the heat of lovemaking had been the sort of trading he'd found himself thinking about.

"Whose name?" he asked gamely. This time, he did reach for the water glass.

The need did not go unnoticed. Megan suppressed a satisfied smile—and a definite ripple through her stomach. "Kathy's boyfriend."

If the revelation surprised him, he gave no indication. "The one you got out of her diary?"

He was on his toes. She would have been disappointed if he hadn't been. "How did you know about her diary?"

Elementary, my dear Watson. "All girls that age have a diary."

Leaning on her upturned hand, Megan looked up at him innocently. "I didn't."

That didn't surprise him in the least. He was beginning to believe that there wasn't anything typical about this woman.

"I don't think you were ever that age, even when you *were* that age."

The observation made Megan laugh. Never mind that it was true: her brother's kidnapping had kidnapped her childhood from her as well. She liked the way he said it. "Are you trying to flatter me, Wichita?"

It was definitely the hour, he decided, but he did like the way she wrapped her tongue around his name. "Depends. How'm I doing?"

Given half a chance, and other circumstances, she might have even liked him. But they were opponents, and she couldn't lose sight of that. He no more wanted to work with her than she wanted to work with him.

But because she was feeling charitable, she gave him his due. *For the moment,* she silently qualified. "So far, you're not turning out to be your typical ugly government agent."

As long as I tell you what you want to know, right Megan? he thought.

Because he had her number, Garrett allowed himself a moment to enjoy the game. "I'll take that as a compliment."

"Good, it was intended as one. So, do you want his name?"

"Sure, why not?" So far, checking out the girl's school and friends had led nowhere. Especially since he'd discovered that everyone he'd talked to had talked to Megan first. It had been a little irritating, following in her shadow. He leaned back in his chair, studying her. "And what is it you want in trade?"

She met his gaze without shifting. "Tell me about Jorge Velasquez."

He kept his expression impassive. Only a slight inflection in his voice hinted at the deeper feelings inside. "He's slime."

And it was personal, Megan realized. Was it just that Wichita was pitting his intellect against the major drug dealer, or was there more?

"I already know that," she acknowledged mildly. "I also know that he's one of the major dealers in cocaine and heroin in the affluent, under-twenty-one set." That was it, she suddenly thought. Wichita had lost someone to Velasquez or drugs, or both. Who? A brother? Sister? Or a girlfriend?

"How is Kathy involved with him?" Megan pressed, her expression growing a little more serious. "The girl seems to be squeaky clean. None of her friends ever saw her with so much as a joint, and there's no hint of her experimenting with drugs on her own."

"You went through her room?" He already knew the answer to that. The lady struck him as thorough.

Megan nodded. "Clean as snow. If that girl parties on anything harder than soda pop, she does it somewhere else."

"Or with someone else," he pointed out.

"Joe Stafford?" It had to have been recent—very recent—or her parents would have suspected something, Megan thought. They had been completely forthcoming about their daughter's habits, and seemed to be on top of everything else when it came to her life.

Joe Stafford. So that was the kid's name, he thought. None of her friends had seemed to know it. They'd said that since Joe had turned up in her life, Kathy had stopped seeing her friends. It wouldn't be the first time that a dominating boyfriend had a strong influence over a girl's life.

Garrett nodded. "That's what I'm thinking."

Megan was accustomed to taking huge leaps from one clue to another. But since she had Wichita here, cooperating, she took baby steps, wanting it all spelled out. "And the tie-in with Velasquez is—?"

"He likes his runners young and naive and eager to please." Just like Andy had been, under that thin bravado of his. "Kathy Teasdale fits all three. And in helping him, the runners suddenly become part of a glamorous world, which would otherwise be off-limits to them." It was her turn now, Garrett thought. "What do you know about this Joe character?"

No one she questioned seemed to know very much about him—not even his brother. Only that he came and went as he pleased—having been expelled from some other high school—and paid his own way. No one was saying how he'd gotten the money to do that.

Megan hedged her answer. It always helped to keep a little back. You never knew when you could use it. "Only that her parents think he's the reason Kathy turned on them."

She wasn't telling him anything new. "A boy is

usually the reason good girls rebel against their parents.''

Megan smiled up into his eyes. They were blue—almost royal blue—and she'd bet they could be spellbinding if he wanted them to be. ''How many good girls rebelled against theirs for you?''

She was definitely not shy and retiring, Garrett thought. And she figured she knew all the right buttons to press. But she'd miscalculated in his case. He had no vanity to appeal to. What appealed to him was honesty. And a beautiful woman. But while the former had lasting power, the latter was only transient.

Like beauty itself, he mused.

Garrett kept a straight face. ''I lost count.''

Megan drew her eyes away from his full mouth, and looked at his eyes again. His mouth made her lose track of her thoughts. But his eyes told her what she wanted to know. That he was putting her on.

A good-looking man who wasn't full of himself. Now there was a novelty. Especially since he was a good-looking man in a position of power. Usually a very lethal combination.

''Bet they didn't,'' she murmured. ''Just a glass of white wine, thanks,'' she told the waiter who had materialized to take her order.

Garrett asked for a French dip sandwich and a glass of red wine. He looked at her as the waiter withdrew. ''Sure I can't interest you in anything else?''

The smile was lazy as it languidly slipped over her lips. Garrett could feel himself reacting to it, even though he knew it was just part of the mental chess game they were engaged in.

''That depends.''

Garrett raised his eyebrow, waiting. "On what?"

Megan couldn't resist. She pushed the wordplay a little further. "On what you have in mind."

Although she knew very well just what it was that he had in mind. Because it was in her mind as well. And if things had been different, maybe…

But they weren't, and she was on a case. And on the opposite side, probably.

He touched his tongue to his teeth, watching her face. "The night is young."

And she bet that he could set it on fire very easily. She felt herself growing antsy. Wistful. It took effort to remember that she was going to walk away from the table and not from his bed.

She would have been lying to herself if she didn't admit that she was tempted to take the latter course. Very, very tempted.

Megan kept her voice cool. "I thought you said you were leaving in the morning."

"Morning is a long way off." And he really wouldn't mind finding her beside him when it arrived.

Garrett looked around. The restaurant was small, intimate. There were a handful of tables scattered about, and a long, elegant bar along one wall.

"Too bad there's no music." He wanted an excuse to hold her. It had been too long since he'd held a woman in his arms. Too long since he'd had time to enjoy himself with one.

Right now, she realized there *was* music. Lots of music. She could hear it clearly in her head. Megan felt herself warming.

"Music is something you carry around inside you." She looked at him significantly.

She was barely aware of the waiter as he returned and set their drinks silently on the table. Picking up her glass, she took a sip of the wine, then looked at Garrett, waiting for his next move.

He almost rose to his feet and took her in his arms to dance, just to see if she would follow through. But then he decided against it. She'd probably just laugh at him for taking the bait.

"Maybe," he allowed. "But if we suddenly get up and start dancing, people might think we're crazy."

"Or in a world of our own." Megan slowly released the breath that she was holding. It seemed absurd that her heart was beating faster, but it was. "I've never concerned myself with what strangers think. I usually never see them again."

They had a lot in common, he thought. It seemed almost a pity that they wouldn't be getting together. But he already knew they wouldn't—not tonight.

Garrett raised his glass to her. "You're a rare woman, Megan Andreini." After a sip, he set his glass down again. "Is that why you went into private investigative work?" He couldn't see her doing anything ordinary. It wouldn't hold her attention for long. "You have to admit, it's not your run-of-the-mill choice for a woman."

She didn't answer his question or comment on his observation. She did, however, clarify it. "I specialize. I find missing children." She avoided the word "look." It implied the possibility of failure—a possibility she refused to entertain.

Reaching into her matching clutch purse, she took out a card and laid it in front of him on the table.

"ChildFinders, Inc.," he read, then raised his eyes to hers. "Rings a bell."

She was very proud of the agency and the reputation she had helped to build. "Someday, it'll set off an entire symphony." She closed her purse. "We have a great track record."

He turned the card over. Hers was the only name on it. "We?"

Megan took another long sip, wondering if it would somehow help deaden the tingling feeling that was taking hold. Instead, it heightened it.

"I have two partners. Sam Walters, and the man who founded the agency, Cade Townsend." Time to push a little more. She leaned closer to him. "So you really believe that Kathy is with Velasquez?"

He wondered if she knew that when she leaned like that, he saw a great deal more of her cleavage than was first evident. He decided that she did. Megan Andreini probably never did anything that wasn't calculated.

Which made Garrett want to find out what it felt like to have her make wild, passionate love with him.

"Yes, I do. At least," he qualified, "she was when that tape was made."

"Five days ago."

Garrett nodded.

He was being honest with her. It was a pleasant surprise that she appreciated. "Seems we have a common goal. Finding Velasquez."

He finished the rest of the wine, and wondered where the waiter was with the rest of his order. She was still looking at him with those green eyes of hers.

"No," he contradicted, knowing that what he was

saying was costing him the rest of the evening. But suddenly, he didn't know if he could keep his perspective if he spent it with her. "We don't. I want to find Velasquez. You want to find Kathy."

The denial surprised her. She had thought he would play out the line a little longer. "But if they're in the same vicinity—"

"I'll make you a deal. When I find Velasquez, if Kathy's still with him, I'll make every effort to keep her safe."

"And my part of the deal?"

He set his mouth hard. The waiter slipped in with Garrett's order, hesitating for a second before setting it down in front of him.

"You stay out of my way," Garrett told her. The waiter took him at his word and hurried off.

"You mean as in 'Don't get in front of me or I'll trip you?' Or as in 'Sit on your hands by a telephone'?"

He knew by her smile that she didn't care for either. "Both."

When hell freezes over, Wichita. I intend to follow you around, step for step.

She looked at him, expressionless. "You don't ask for much, do you?"

He glanced at his order, but didn't pick it up. "I always try to be reasonable."

"Keep trying," she murmured.

Garrett looked at her sharply. "What was that?"

Megan finished her drink before answering. She wasn't about to get anything further out of him tonight, she thought. He was determined to be a tight-lipped, pompous ass. "I think it's past my bedtime."

A sense of loss doused him, even though he'd expected that things would turn out this way. "I've got a bed upstairs. Save you a trip home."

Megan smiled, turning down the invitation. Turning away from the temptation.

"I'd only have to go home in the morning. Might as well not put things off." She rose to her feet. "But thanks for the offer."

He rose as well, coaxed to his feet by an appetite that insisted on plaguing him. "Speaking of not putting things off—"

"Yes?"

Because he was good at what he did, he figured there was more than an even chance that he wouldn't see her again—at least not soon. Nothing ventured, nothing gained.

"I've been wondering what it would be like to kiss you."

Megan wouldn't have been able to explain just why she felt as if someone had suddenly put a match to her. But she did.

She raised her face slightly, challenging him. "So what's keeping you from finding out?"

"Not a thing," he murmured.

Chapter 4

Megan could feel her heart hammering wildly in her chest like a carpenter out of control. Could feel the rhythm echoing in her throat and her ears.

It was ridiculous, absolutely ridiculous, to feel this way. She was a grown woman.

Maybe, a tiny voice whispered, *you're feeling this way* because *you're a grown woman.*

She couldn't take her eyes off his, even as he slipped his hands along her face, tilting it up toward him. Even as he lowered his mouth to hers.

Her breathing stopped.

The hammering didn't.

Over the years, she'd lost track of how many times she'd kissed and been kissed. Precocious, she'd started out on the road early, when she was barely thirteen, with a game of Spin the Bottle. Kissing had always been enjoyable—even pleasurable—with the right partner.

But she'd never before felt anticipation stop the air moving in her lungs.

Well, except for the first time. And that had been a huge disappointment.

Just like this was probably going to be.

A feeling of heated curiosity slowly forged its way through his veins, and Garrett cupped her face and touched his lips to hers.

She tasted of wine and promise. And of sins yet uncommitted.

Intrigued, looking for bottom, Garrett deepened the kiss. And found there was no bottom. Only an overwhelming sense of wonder.

Curiosity took him prisoner.

The napkin she'd forgotten to leave on the table slid from her fingers to the floor. Before she realized what she was doing, Megan had dug her fingertips into his shoulders, for balance.

And to keep from being swept away.

Struggling for air, for her own depth, knowing she'd be lost if she didn't do something immediately in self-defense, she kissed him back. Long and hard.

And disintegrated his kneecaps. Both of them. He could feel them going in unison. Garrett could have sworn he heard thunder roaring in his ears as well.

He wanted more.

An intrusive noise, occurring somewhere along the perimeter of this world that contained only two, finally registered. It forced Garrett to draw away from the feisty little private investigator with the wicked, wicked mouth and the seductive attitude. Their waiter was clearing his throat, making his presence known as politely as possible.

Releasing Megan, Garrett looked at the man expectantly. The waiter looked straight him, his face sober, as if he hadn't interrupted anything unusual.

"Will there be anything else, sir?"

Yeah, there was going to be something else. But not here and not now, Garrett thought. But there *was* going to be something else. He made that promise to himself.

Garrett tested his throat by clearing it first. It was a wonder she hadn't disintegrated his vocal cords, he thought. His eyes shifted to Megan. "Dessert?"

She almost laughed at the deadpan. "I've already had mine."

"Yeah, me too." He looked at the waiter. "You can bring the check."

Megan stepped back, surprised that she still could. For a second there, her legs had felt as wobbly as gelatin. Uncertainty took a toehold. Wichita looked as if he was getting ready to go upstairs—with her. But suddenly, she wasn't ready to continue the game. Not just yet.

"Don't leave on my account." She nodded at his plate, already distancing herself from the table. And from him. "Enjoy your French dip," she said over her shoulder. Then she walked away.

He would rather have enjoyed *her*.

Business first, pleasure later, he warned himself. He

remained where he was, watching her go. It was a moment longer before he trusted his legs enough to attempt to sit down. He didn't want to embarrass himself by collapsing into the chair.

The lady, he mused as she disappeared from view, was every bit as lethal as she looked.

"And you kissed him."

His voice ringing with disbelief and amusement, Sam Walters crossed his arms in front of his chest and leaned back against the edge of Megan's desk. Well, well, well. He had to admit to himself that this certainly was an interesting footnote to her narrative.

Megan frowned at his tone. She'd come in early, hoping not to find anyone at the office. There were several things she wanted to check out before she got back to the Teasdales. She wanted to do it without interruptions.

But her plans evaporated when she discovered that both Sam and Cade were already there. Working on separate cases, all three of them had independently chosen to start at seven a.m.

Sam, winding up his own case, had wanted to know how hers was going. She found herself fielding one question after another.

In an unguarded moment, because last night had left her a little shaken and bemused, she'd told him what had happened in the restaurant.

Turning away from the computer, she dragged her hand through her hair. "Yes, he kissed me."

She dearly regretted having slipped and told him

this. She shared a lot with Sam, but this kind of thing wasn't supposed to be on the agenda. The very fact that telling him bothered her upset Megan even more. It made the moment—the kiss—out to be something more important that it was.

She and Sam had been friends ever since tenth grade. It was she who had brought Sam into the agency. Megan was as close to him as she ever allowed herself to be to anyone. For all intents and purposes, Sam was family.

And right now, he was annoying.

Sam had to admit that he was amazed. More than once, he'd seen Megan weave her webs when she was after something, but he'd never known her to get tangled up in the threads before. This was something new.

"Right in front of everybody?" He was trying to picture it in his mind. It didn't quite jibe with the private Megan he knew.

Sam glanced up to see that Cade was standing in the doorway. One-quarter Cherokee, one-quarter Navajo, there were times when Sam thought the man seemed to be part spirit, materializing before anyone knew he was there. Sam's guess was that Cade had heard everything that Megan had to say about the runaway case.

"I was only trying to get information out of Wichita. Is that clear?"

"A lip-to-lip transfer." Sam nodded his head sagely. "Must be something new." He looked over his shoulder toward the doorway. "You hear about it, Cade?"

There was just the slightest hint of a smile on Cade's mouth. "News to me."

Terrific. Now she had both of them in here, acting like annoying little brothers. She glared at Sam. It served her right for sharing anything.

"This is the last time I answer any questions around here." Sam laughed in response, and even Cade allowed himself a full smile. She gave up. "You two are hopeless. You know that, don't you?"

Cade crossed to her, laying a friendly hand on her shoulder.

"Never hopeless, Megan. Always hopeful," he corrected. It was a motto he lived by. Until he found his son, he had no other choice but to embrace it. "So where do you go from here?"

Because Cade's only real rule at the agency was to be informed about the cases they undertook and then to keep at least nominally apprised of strategy and progress, Megan had already dashed off a quick note about her plans.

Since he was asking her, she assumed he hadn't seen the note yet.

She glanced at the last screen she'd pulled up on the monitor. She was logged on to the Missing and Abused Children web site. There was nothing listed here, either. No one had bothered to input any data on Joe Stafford. She supposed that since he'd turned eighteen recently, he no longer qualified as a missing child.

That didn't mean he wasn't one.

With a sigh, she closed the program.

"I'm going to go back to the Teasdales to find out

if any of their credit cards are missing.'' Garrett's appearance at their house yesterday had made her forget to ask about that. She upbraided herself for the oversight. And for her response to him. That made two things she held against him. "Maybe there's a paper trail I can follow. If all else fails, I intend to tail Wichita.''

There'd been something in her eyes when she mentioned the DEA agent that had given Sam pause. If anyone had asked, he would have said that Garrett Wichita had better watch his back.

Still, Sam couldn't resist. "Liked communicating with him that much, did you?''

Her frown deepened. "Can it, Sammy. Just because we're supposed to be friends doesn't mean I can't use you for target practice.'' She looked at Cade. At least she could always depend on him to be serious, and she proceeded to fill him in on Kathy's association with Velasquez.

With her former FBI training, Cade knew that Megan could take care of herself, but that didn't stop him from being concerned about her. "Her parents know?''

She laughed shortly. "No, thank goodness.'' They were worried enough as it was. News like this could kill them. "From what Wichita said, I don't think Kathy really knows what she's involved in. According to him, Velasquez likes them naive and innocent and underage.''

The phone rang. Sam, who was closest to it, leaned over and picked up the receiver. "ChildFinders, Inc.

How can I help you?'' It was an opening phrase that had brought so many cases into their lives in the last two-and-a-half years. And to Sam, it had brought more. It had brought Savannah and her daughter, Aimee, and forever changed his life for the better.

He paused now, listening. A look of recognition came over his face, and his eyes shifted to Megan.

''She's right here. Why don't you tell her yourself?'' Putting his hand over the mouthpiece, Sam quietly said to Megan, ''I think you just got your first break.'' He held out the receiver to her.

She had no idea what he was talking about, but she had a pretty good idea she knew who had to be on the other end of the line.

''Hello?''

She heard Judith Teasdale's breathless voice in her ear, slightly muffled and indistinct. Megan's guess was that the woman had been crying. Was probably crying still. She remembered coming up on her mother.

Don't cry, Mommy, please don't cry.

I can't help it, Megan. The tears just won't stop coming.

''Megan, she called,'' Judith was saying. ''Kathy called—'' Her voice broke. It was a moment before she could continue. Megan heard the woman say, ''No, I'm not all right, how could I be?'' and knew that Warren was there with his wife. ''Kathy's in terrible trouble,'' Judith told her. ''I just know it.''

It didn't take an expert to see that Judith was on the verge of becoming incoherent. The stress was beginning to tear her apart.

"Calm down, Mrs. Teasdale." Megan kept her own voice steady, though it wasn't easy. If Kathy had made contact, there was a strong chance that the case could all be wrapped up before the weekend. "What did she say to you? Try to remember her exact words."

She heard Judith draw a deep breath before saying, "Her exact words were 'Help me, Mom.'"

Megan could hear Judith's voice filling with tears again. She had to keep the woman focused. "Did she tell you where she was?"

"No, no she didn't. She was talking crazy. Crying. Megan, I've never heard her like that. I couldn't make any sense out of what she was saying. She kept apologizing, telling me she was sorry. Asking her father and me to forgive her. Said she didn't know what she was doing, and now it was too late. She was afraid," Judith said, sobbing. "Very, very afraid. I tried to tell her that it wasn't too late, that it was never too late. That we'd come and get her—her father and I. All she had to do was tell me where she was. But she wouldn't. That was when she said that he'd kill us if we came for her."

Megan thought she knew who Kathy was referring to, but for Judith's sake, she played dumb. "'He'?"

For a moment, Megan debated putting the call on the speaker phone so the others could also hear, then decided against it. She didn't want any extraneous sound throwing the woman off.

"I guess she must have meant Joe. I tried to reason with her, to tell her that we would handle everything. All she had to do was tell us where to find her. The last thing she said was that she couldn't. And then she hung up." Judith began sobbing. "How can I help her, Megan, if I can't get to her?"

Wichita had asked permission for a tap. It had to be in place by now. If she were to make a calculated guess, Megan would say that the machinery had already been in place and running when he'd asked the Teasdales' permission yesterday.

"How long was Kathy on the phone with you?"

With obvious effort, Judith collected herself. "Not long. She talked very quickly. At first, I didn't even know that it was Kathy. It just didn't sound like my baby."

Megan guessed that the teenager was probably coming off a high, or about to take flight, and had clutched to the last ounce of common sense and courage she had in order to make the call.

"What did he do to her, Megan?" Judith demanded.

Nothing irreversible, I hope.

"First we get her back, then we sort out everything else," Megan promised. "You did very well, calling me, Mrs. Teasdale. Let me talk to your husband, please." She heard the receiver being transferred, then Warren's deep voice came on the line.

"Megan?"

"Hello, Mr. Teasdale. Don't talk, just listen. I hate to add to your concerns, but if you have any kind of a tranquilizer in the house, I'd suggest you have your wife take it. Not enough to knock her out, just enough to calm her down a little. Do you understand? She sounds on the verge of a breakdown."

There was pain in Warren's voice. "You're right, she is. I'll see what I can find."

"Great. I'll see you in a little while. One more thing—can you remember what time Kathy called?"

"Just a few minutes ago. We called you immediately after she hung up."

Glancing at her watch, Megan approximated the time and jotted it down.

Shouldn't be a problem pinpointing the call, she mused. What would be a problem was getting the DEA to share the information. But that was what connections and unreturned favors were for.

"Thank you." She put down her pencil. "Hang in there, Mr. Teasdale. It's almost over."

Hanging up, she looked at Cade and Sam. Neither one had moved since the call had come in. It was great, she thought, knowing you had a support group always watching your back. Knowing you had people you could always count on. Her mouth curved. Even if the "group" only consisted of two guys.

Megan leaned back in her chair. "Okay, who do we know in the DEA or with connections to the DEA?"

"Why?" Cade asked. "What's up?"

She'd already filled Sam in on Garrett's background. She didn't know how much Cade had overheard.

"They have a phone tap on the Teasdales' phone. Had it there since yesterday. That means when her call came in, they got a lock on the general location, if not the actual number. To get that location, we need someone on the inside. Wichita doesn't strike me as someone who willingly plays well with others and shares, unless there's something in it for him."

Cade shook his head. "The DEA is a little out of my league." He'd been a writer before opening ChildFinders, Inc. Megan and Sam were the ones with law enforcement connections.

"Sam?" she said.

Sam appeared dubious. "I'll make a few calls, but nobody comes to mind right off the bat." He looked at Megan. "I always thought government agents were your realm, Megan."

"I never got into that part of the alphabet," she quipped, frustrated. "Why don't you make your calls?" She pushed the telephone toward Sam.

He picked up the receiver, then thought of his wife and the way he'd met her. When Savannah had come to him, asking him to locate her kidnapped daughter, she'd only made one stipulation. She'd wanted to come along with him on the investigation.

Holding the telephone receiver aloft, his fingers poised over the keypad, he looked at Megan. "I've got another idea."

Garrett sighed, feeling more dead than alive. He'd spent the night seeking peaceful oblivion on every part of the damn mattress, only to fail.

You'd think by now, after all this time, he would have become accustomed to sleeping in strange places. He'd done it for more than half his life, both privately and on the job.

But it seemed that the only place he actually got a

decent night's sleep was in that small two-bedroom house he had bought five years ago and made his home.

Everywhere else left him tossing and turning, wired and restless at the same time. And, like as not, feeling like hell. He supposed, if he looked at it in a positive light, feeling wired gave him an edgy energy that the job made adequate use of.

Still, it would have been nice to get out of bed in the morning feeling as if he were actually rested and relaxed, instead of as if he were a warmed-over plate of stew.

A shower would help a little. Garrett walked off to the bathroom.

Ten minutes later, the receiver was in his hand, still vibrating from its first ring. His body was still dripping from the shower. The fact that the temperature in the hotel room was too hot didn't help matters any. It had been that way, he discovered, ever since he'd come up here last night. Alone and thinking of Megan. And what had happened between them.

And what hadn't.

He ran his hand through his hair, sending drops of water scattering. A drop fell into his eye, and he blinked it away.

"Wichita here."

"Good news, Garrett." It was Oscar. He should have known. "That lost sheep you're looking for called home this morning."

"Got a location?" He riffled through the nightstand

drawer for paper and pencil, but found none. He'd have to trust his memory for details.

"Got a city," Oscar answered brightly. "Best we could do. The girl hung up before Carlucci could get a final lock on the call."

The name of the DEA agent was unfamiliar to him, but Garrett let it go. There were more important questions. "How big a city?"

Oscar paused. "Big."

That meant one of the major ones. Well, they already knew that their man got around. Garrett let the towel drop on the floor and cradling the receiver against his neck, hurriedly pulled on his pants. "Great."

Oscar wasn't put off by the tone. "Hey, you can't have everything. Then there'd be no challenge. Guess where you're headed off to?"

Barefoot, Garrett hunted around for his shoes. "Skip the guessing games, Oscar. Just tell me where. I'm not in the mood to play."

Oscar laughed. Garrett could see the man's more than ample belly shaking. "Whose wrong side of the bed did you wake up on this morning?"

Megan's face involuntarily intruded on his thoughts. He deliberately shut it out again.

"Nobody's."

"Well, that would explain it." He laughed again as Garrett growled a warning at him. Oscar sobered. He knew when to stop playing. "You're off to Scottsdale my friend."

"Scottsdale?" Finding his shoes, Garrett sat down

on the bed and put his socks on quickly. Belatedly, he looked down to see if they matched. They did. "Isn't that like the Beverly Hills of Arizona?"

"Yeah. Nothing but the best for our drug dealer," Oscar cracked.

"No, he *feeds* on nothing but the best," Garrett corrected grimly. And Andy had been the best. Before he'd gotten lost. "How long a trip is that?"

Picking up his suitcase from the floor, Garrett tossed it on the bed. Except for a change of clothes, he hadn't unpacked anything. In the last year, he hadn't been anywhere long enough to make use of a closet.

"Roughly three hundred miles as the crow flies."

Garrett frowned, unzipping a false compartment in the bottom of the suitcase and checking his ammunition. "How long is it if the crow's driving a car?"

"Oh, yeah, right. I forgot our man doesn't fly."

Velasquez had a pathological fear of airplanes. Garrett dreamed of taking the drug dealer up over an empty field and giving him his first skydiving lesson. "No, only his customers do."

"Hang on, I'll print up a route and fax it to you."

In the background, the radio he'd turned on to keep him company in the room had Willie Nelson singing "On the Road Again."

It was quickly becoming his own theme song, Garrett thought. He would have preferred another.

Garrett dragged out another suitcase, a smaller one this time. "Hang on while I hook up the portable fax."

"All the comforts of home, eh, Garrett?"

Garrett glanced around at the impersonal room with

its torture rack of a bed. He remembered the string of foster homes that had littered his teen years. This was preferable to that.

"Yeah."

Chapter 5

Hurrying through the revolving doors of the Random Hotel, Megan quickly scanned the lobby. She hoped she wasn't too late. Even though it wasn't even nine o'clock, something told her that Garrett liked getting an early start.

Halfway to the front desk, she sighted her target. Garrett was standing by the front desk with his back to her, two small carry-on suitcases on the floor on either side of him.

Bingo.

From the looks of it, her hunch was right. She'd gotten here just in time. Coming closer, she saw that his hair looked damp. The call from headquarters must have pulled him right out of the shower. An image of Garrett, dripping wet and toweling himself off, popped unbidden into her head. Megan tried not to dwell on it.

Sam had promised to call her on her cell phone if he tracked down any leads on Kathy's call. So far, her phone hadn't rung. That meant Wichita was her only key.

She didn't like putting all her eggs in one basket.

She'd been almost at the hotel when she remembered that she'd told the Teasdales that she was on her way to their house. Megan had placed a quick call to the couple to let them know of the change in plans, and that she was currently on her way to see if she could trace Kathy's call.

On impulse, Megan had asked Warren to call the number that the DEA agent had given him. There was an outside chance that Wichita would actually release the location of the incoming call to Kathy's father.

It was worth a try, though she doubted that Wichita would be willing to be straightforward with the couple. The man had struck her as someone who was too wound up around winning his case to remember that there were real people involved in it, every step of the way. People like the Teasdales, who were getting their hearts kicked in—all because they'd tried to live a decent life, and loved their daughter.

But you never knew. Stranger things had happened.

Catching her breath now, Megan came up behind Wichita. "You really were serious about checking out early, weren't you?"

Garrett stopped writing his name on the credit slip, as the sound of her voice sank in. Completing the signature, he laid down the pen and turned around to look at her. If he thought about it, he wasn't really all that surprised to find her standing there.

The lady was in for a rude awakening. His hands were tied. He couldn't tell her any more than he'd told Warren Teasdale, when the man had called a few minutes ago.

"I never say what I don't mean," Garrett finally said, taking back his credit card from the clerk. His eyes on Megan, he carefully inserted the card into his wallet.

Garrett half expected Megan to still be wearing her clingy turquoise dress. The tan jeans and bright green pullover were admittedly a bit of a letdown.

But when he raised his eyes to her face, she still had that come-hither look in her eyes, and he remembered what that mouth had tasted like.

He should have taken a cold shower instead of a hot one, he decided. Too late now.

Gamely, Megan decided to test his honesty, at least as far as this situation went. She bet Wichita said a great many things that he didn't mean, given the right situations. Or the wrong ones, depending on your take on things. "I suppose you know that Kathy Teasdale called her parents this morning."

"Did she now?" he asked dryly.

There was no point in appearing surprised. It would just be a waste of time. She'd been standing right there when he'd asked the Teasdales for permission to tap their line.

Ignoring his amused expression, she pressed on. "And I suppose you know where the call came from."

He picked up a suitcase in each hand, shook his head at the bellman, and began walking toward the revolving doors. "There's a fifty-fifty chance you might be right."

Fifty-fifty chance, my foot. "And I suppose," she continued, raising her voice to be heard as they both went through the hotel's revolving door, "that you're not about to share that information with me."

Coming out behind him, she rapped a knee against one of his suitcases. Megan bit her lower lip to keep from making a sound.

Garrett grinned at her as he looked over his shoulder. "There's a better chance of you being right about that."

She thought as much.

Garrett widened his stride.

As she hurried to keep up with him, Megan realized that he was bypassing the parking valet and going straight to the self-parking structure. She'd parked her own car across the street in what she hoped was the spot with the best view of the hotel's parking lot. It looked now as if her foresight was going to pay off; she had a strong feeling that he wasn't going to go for what she had in mind.

"What do you think about us temporarily teaming up?"

He spared her a look that was far from flattering. "You really don't want to know the answer to that." Picking up his pace, he left her behind.

"I wouldn't have asked if I didn't," she called after him. He made no answer.

The DEA agent was carrying two suitcases, and the path to the parking structure was slanted slightly upward, but the man didn't slow; he was in great shape. But she'd already figured that part out last night at the restaurant.

Annoyed now, Megan all but trotted to cut the space between them.

Wichita took the stairs to the second level rather than the elevator.

It figured. She was going to have to see about getting back to her tae kwan do exercises, Megan promised herself. Right after she finished up this case.

And him.

"Hey, Wichita, wait up."

When he made no effort to stop or even slow down, she raced after him. Her opinion about his direct connection to the missing link became stronger.

Because she was hurrying, Megan almost plowed straight into his back, when Garrett abruptly stopped beside a four-door sedan. Recovering, she bit off a few ripe words about his manners. She could save that for later.

Stepping back, she looked at the car. It was probably the last vehicle she would have pictured him driving. He belonged behind the wheel of something sleek, racy.

Dusty, bland, with two dents in the front fender, this car looked as if it had known a far better decade than this one. It definitely did not look like a car belonging to a man who could disintegrate your knees with one kiss.

Bemused and curious, she surveyed the back end of the car. There was another dent—a larger one, right in the center of the bumper. Had someone played road tag with him?

She raised her eyes questioningly to his. "What's the matter, Wichita? The department doesn't pay you enough to buy a decent car?"

He ignored the disparaging look on her face. "It's a rental." And it had been the only thing available at the time. He'd learned a long time ago to make the best of whatever happened his way.

"It's not a rental, it's a wreck," she countered. But she wasn't here to talk about his choice in cars. Megan moved in front of him, as he slipped his hand into his pocket for the keys. "Look, why can't we team up and share information? What harm would it do?"

Garrett looked at her. She had no idea, did she? Having her nosing around could blow the case right out from under him. And maybe get her runaway killed as well. The woman was a liability looking to happen.

"Potentially, a lot. I don't have time to stand here and discuss it with you."

"Got a plane to catch?"

He wished. And then it occurred to him that if he led her to the tangled web of parking lots at John Wayne Airport, she'd think he was at the airport somewhere, rather than driving to Scottsdale.

He looked down at Megan, purposely tight-lipped.
"Maybe."

"Wouldn't want to tell me which airline, would
you?"

"No, I wouldn't."

Taking out his key, Garrett unlocked the trunk and
threw in one of the suitcases. He reached for the second one, but Megan already had it. Annoyance took
hold. He expected her to do something infantile, like
using it to barter with.

But she surprised him by depositing it into his trunk
behind the first suitcase.

Did she think that she could ingratiate herself that
simply? Maybe she wasn't as bright as she seemed.
"Hey, you don't have to—"

As she turned against him, the strap of Megan's
oversize bag slid off her shoulder and fell at his feet.
Frowning, he swallowed his admonishment and bent
down to pick it up, then shoved it unceremoniously
into her hands.

"There, we're even," he pronounced. "Now if
you'll just step out of the way, there's someplace that
I have to be."

And Megan meant to be there with him, or behind
him. She'd just seen to it. But if she didn't protest,
he'd be suspicious. "Wichita—"

Garrett blew out an exasperated breath. "All right,
have it your way."

Hands on either side of her shoulders, Garrett lifted
her quickly off the ground and moved her to the side.

Depositing her again, he strode to the driver's side and got in.

He half expected her to tear around the hood and jump in the passenger side. Instead, he heard Megan mutter something marginally unflattering about him under her breath. Then, as he watched in the side mirror, he saw Megan turn on her heel and quickly walk away.

For a second, he just sat there, staring. He had to admit that the jeans looked a hell of a lot better from this view.

And then she was gone.

Slipping the key in the ignition, he started up the car. After an initial cough, it came to life. But he hardly noticed; his mind lingered on Megan.

Well, that had certainly turned out to be a lot easier than he'd expected. He'd obviously given her too much credit and overestimated her tenacity. Too bad the rest of the case couldn't arrange itself like that for him.

Still, he couldn't quite shake the feeling that he wasn't really in the clear.

Just because you're paranoid... he mused.

When Garrett finally drove out of the parking structure, he scanned the surrounding area slowly, looking for Megan. She didn't appear to be anywhere in sight.

Maybe this was too easy, he decided.

To be on the safe side, he drove the car the half-mile to the airport, and then spent the next fifteen minutes weaving in and out of the various terminal-designated parking lots, just in case she was following him.

He never saw her.

Satisfied, Garrett hit the road again, heading for the state line.

Flying would have been faster, but Velasquez traveled everywhere in his white stretch limousine. The hassle of checking in and out of airports and renting cars only unnecessarily ate into Garrett's margin of operation.

His superior, Jim Cassidy, had once told him that you had to live like your quarry in order to catch him. Garrett had asked Cassidy if that meant he had to surround himself with white furnishings and wear white suits the way Velasquez did. Cassidy had replied something that couldn't have been put in any report.

But Cassidy had held fast to the belief that Garrett had to drive rather than fly, so Garrett drove, and occupied himself by reviewing information that would eventually put the nails into Velasquez's legal coffin.

Several times along the road during the six-hour trip that followed, Garrett looked in his rearview mirror to check out the road behind him. But the cars that were following him were always different from ones that had been there the last time he'd looked.

Sighing, he felt vaguely disappointed. It made no sense to Garrett, and he didn't even bother trying to understand it.

The cell phone lying on the seat beside him rang just as he entered the Scottsdale city limits. He welcomed the break. It was a wonder that he hadn't fallen asleep, traveling through monotonous vast stretches of nothing but cacti and country that only hermits could have enjoyed.

He flipped the telephone open and held it to his ear. "Talk to me."

"No 'hello'? No 'How are you, Oscar?'"

"You're getting to sound like a wife, Oscar." Garrett laughed, shaking his head. "One of us has been at this too long."

There was no hesitation. "Must be you. I've already got a wife. I've also got an address for you, so be nice to me."

Any sleepiness induced by long miles of desert terrain vanished. Every bone in his body tensed. "Velasquez's?"

"None other."

The odds had been less than fifteen percent in their favor that any informant on the street had the address. There was still a chance that it was bogus, a plant. Ninety percent of the job was tracking down false leads and working trails that went nowhere.

"I'll name my firstborn after you—now give me the address."

"I'll hold you to that." Oscar read off the numbers and street name, and gave the cross streets. Pulling over to the side on the hilly road, Garrett wrote everything down. "I could fax a street map," Oscar offered.

"Not necessary." He'd thought to buy a road map at the last gas station. The map looked fairly old, but appeared reliable enough. Garrett looked at the address before folding the paper and putting it in his pocket. "Where did you get this?"

"Comes by way of one of the disgruntled locals. Claims the drugs Velasquez gave him to distribute were poor quality. When he went to complain, Velasquez threatened to have him cut up for shark bait. Now he's hiding from both the small-time dealers and Velasquez's people. The snitch traded the address for protection."

It was a familiar song, only a few of the lyrics were different. Garrett released his emergency brake and got back on the road.

"Hope they put someone good on it. Velasquez likes his revenge." And the man, they all knew, had a knack of getting his way.

"Want backup?" Oscar asked. "I can tell Cassidy—"

"No, not yet." Garrett didn't want egg on his face if this did turn out to be a false lead. He and Cassidy had already had words. He wasn't about to be the reason twenty DEA agents swarmed the wrong house. "Let me check it out first, and then I'll get back to you."

"Okay, partner." Oscar sounded doubtful. "Just don't do anything stupid."

"You got it, Mother." Garrett rang off before Oscar had a chance to answer, then smiled to himself. He supposed that Oscar was as close to him as he'd allowed anyone to get in the last fifteen years. Since Andy had died.

"Maybe Velasquez is finally going to get his, big brother," Garrett murmured as he followed the windy, hilly road to the address Oscar had given him.

He could see why Velasquez had chosen this location, however temporarily. From up here, his drivers could catch anyone coming from the opposite direction off guard, and force them over the side.

Tension rode up the hill with him.

There was another reason that the dealer had probably chosen the house, Garrett thought as he approached it. Perched at the top of the hill, it looked down at the affluent city below. The city beneath its feet. It fit in with the way Velasquez pictured himself—lording it over the rest of humanity.

"What goes up, must come down," Garrett murmured, relishing the dealer's coming fall.

Hiding the car behind a tangle of mesquite that grew tall and wild, he quickly made his way toward the house. Garrett was exposed, but he was counting on the fact that no one was looking his way at that moment. Luck had kept him alive this long.

The house, running about six-thousand square feet, by Garrett's guess, had gleaming white stucco walls and recessed windows, and looked at first to be a fortress. That was also in keeping with Velasquez's image, he thought.

There was an eerie stillness surrounding the house. Not even the wind was stirring.

The calm before the storm?

Garrett knew his quarry well enough not to let his guard down, no matter how peaceful everything seemed. *If* Velasquez was here. So far, there was no evidence of anyone being around.

There were no cars in the driveway, not even the trademark white stretch limousine. No loud music coming from the windows, opened now to let in the early evening air. Garrett knew Velasquez liked his music blaring and fast, just like his women.

He saw no evidence of either.

It was beginning to seem as though someone had given them the wrong address.

Very slowly, like a soldier on patrol in enemy territory, Garrett made his way around to the perimeter of the house. Every foot was surrounded by tall saguaros, each with arms that were extended on either side like deadly green sentries. The hoary cacti spines looked more lethal than a moat filled with alligators.

The cacti made looking through the windows difficult, but using a pair of miniature binoculars, he managed. And found that there was no one there.

Something felt wrong.

Garrett drew his gun out of his holster. In the distance, on the far side of the building, something shiny suddenly caught his eye. He couldn't see what it was because of the shrubs that were in the way. Whatever gleamed was up high enough to be the hood of a car.

Was he being watched and toyed with for Velasquez's entertainment?

A trickle of perspiration shimmied down his back.

As Garrett came around to the front, he looked through the window and saw the body. Lean, dressed in black, the figure was sprawled out facedown on the pristine white sofa. It looked to be a man, but he couldn't be sure.

Garrett swallowed a curse. He needed to get inside the house.

The garage and front door were the only accessible places. He opted for the garage. Still taking precautions, Garrett short-circuited the garage door opener, and let himself in. The cavernous area was completely deserted.

Looks like Elvis has left the building, he thought, frustration eating away at him.

Every nerve ending was sensitive, tense, as Garrett slowly made his way into the living room. And then stopped dead.

There was a blonde bending over the body.

Chapter 6

"What the hell are you doing here?"

Pressing two fingers against the teenager's throat to find a pulse, Megan jerked her head up at the barked question. Finding the teenager had momentarily made her forget about the DEA agent she'd been tailing.

She felt the faintest of flutters beneath her fingertips. Relief branched through her. At least the boy wasn't dead. Yet.

But even as she thought it, she felt the flutter in his throat disappear. His pulse was gone. Damn.

Megan quickly pushed the boy flat onto the sofa, then with one hand over the other she began to press hard on his chest.

"Following you," she said, looking in Garrett's direction as he crossed to her.

"Following me?" he echoed. "How can you be following me? You're here ahead of me."

"Correction." Pinching the boy's nose, Megan breathed into his mouth. Something pungent and repelling assaulted her nose. What had he consumed? "I got here after you did." Breathing out through her mouth, she forced air into his lungs again. "I just hit the living room before you did."

"I didn't see anyone following me."

Was she part of this? he suddenly wondered. He looked at Megan in a completely different light. Was she just posing as a private investigator to throw him off, while she was actually part of the muck and slime that was Velasquez's organization?

But if that were true, what was her advantage? If Velasquez was onto him, he'd be dead by now.

Working furiously over the teenager's chest again, Megan shot Garrett an exasperated look. "You weren't supposed to see me."

She caught his expression. Wichita was looking at her strangely, as if he didn't believe her. As if he were having doubts about her altogether. The suspicion in his eyes was on the verge of turning into something ugly, but she didn't have time to deal with that right now. She was losing a battle.

"Live, damn you," she cried, hitting the teenager's chest with the flat of her hand.

To her relief, she saw it respond ever so slightly. He was breathing on his own again. Her heart racing, Megan pushed her hair out of her eyes, and spared

Garrett an annoyed look. A lot of help *he'd* turned out to be.

The look on his face was still there.

He thought she was one of them, she realized. Megan knew she had to share something with him in order to get back to level footing with the agent. Otherwise, it was hopeless.

"I put a transponder in your car."

Garrett's eyes narrowed. He'd watched her closely this morning. She hadn't had the time to bug his car. "When?" he demanded.

She slid onto the sofa beside the unconscious boy. Dressed all in black, he looked like a tall pipe cleaner. A half-dead pipe cleaner.

"When you gallantly picked up my shoulder bag, I put the device inside your trunk. I let you play hide-and-seek all by yourself in the airport parking lots, although I have to admit that you surprised me when you kept on going." It hadn't made any sense to her then, and it still didn't. "Why didn't you just fly here?"

Unprepared for the extensive road trip, Megan had had to pull into a gas station before continuing. The traffic jam that engulfed her just before she crossed the California-Arizona line had caused her to lose his signal. She'd kept on traveling in good faith for more than half an hour before she picked it up again.

Garrett wasn't inclined to explain himself, but since she'd told him about the transmitter, he grudgingly made an exception.

"Velasquez doesn't fly. It increases chances of our

paths crossing.'' He frowned. ''Never mind that now. You're not supposed to be here. You're impeding a federal investigation.''

Dragging her hand through her hair, she looked at the unconscious boy.

''Way I see it, I'm not impeding anything. I just saved his life.'' To prove it, she took Garrett's fingers and pressed them against the boy's neck, so he could feel the pulse for himself. ''It's faint,'' she said before he could comment. ''We need to get him to hospital. Now.''

Sliding his hand away from hers, Garrett turned toward the telephone on the coffee table. White—like everything else in the room—with a curved receiver, it was shaped to resemble an old-fashioned telephone, complete with rotary dial. Velasquez liked to surround himself with graceful things.

Leaning over, Megan grabbed the cuff of his sleeve to stop him. ''There isn't time to wait for an ambulance to get here.''

With his thumb over the teenager's eyelid, Garrett raised it to see the bloodshot eye beneath. She was right. He would have realized it himself if seeing her here hadn't completely thrown him. It looked as if the teenager had overdosed.

Garrett let the lid drop. ''Do you know what you're talking about?''

Since it was phrased as a question rather than an accusation, Megan took no offense. ''I've had a course in EMS—Emergency Medical Services,'' she clarified when he merely looked at her. Unable to resist, she added, "And I usually know what I'm talking about. It looks like he partied just a little too much."

"Or that's what they want anyone who happens to find him to think."

By "they," Megan knew he was talking about the drug ring. A sense of urgency pervaded Megan. She had to find Kathy before anything happened to the girl.

On her feet, Megan struggled to get her shoulder under the teenager's arm. He had a good six inches on her, if not more, and all of it was dead weight. She glared at Garrett. "You could try helping."

"I figured you were just going to throw him over your shoulder and fly out of here." In his opinion, the woman had a definite superhero complex.

Before she could retort, he moved her aside and picked the boy up in his arms as easily as if he were picking up a pile of clothes. The boy lay just as limply in his arms.

Megan grabbed her purse and hurried after them. She knew Garrett was not about to slow down for her benefit.

But when he came to the front door, he had to stop. It was closed. Megan reached around him to get the doorknob, brushing against his midsection as she did so.

Their eyes met for less than a second. Just long enough for each to acknowledge that contact with the other was noted. And felt.

She opened the door for him, stepping back. "Has he done this before? Velasquez, I mean."

Garrett didn't even look at her. The woman had

been privy to more than he'd wanted her to be as it was. Instead, carrying the teenager in his arms, he strode to his car. Her question brought a volley of statistics crowding into his mind. "More than once. With anyone who's outlived their usefulness."

"He doesn't look as if he's had enough time to outlive anything."

"He has if he's eighteen and had nothing else to offer Velasquez beyond his age."

Though Megan thought of herself as fairly hardened, the situation was beginning to get to her. If the boy died, it would be such a pathetic waste. And Wichita was talking as matter-of-factly as if he were reciting some formula out of a textbook.

Megan threw open the passenger door for Garrett. "Do all DEA people talk in sound bites?"

Garrett deposited the boy in the front seat, then strapped him in before answering.

"When Velasquez's couriers turn eighteen, they become a liability to him. They can be tried as adults. That leaves the door open to plea bargaining and testimonies in exchange for immunity—areas he doesn't want to risk leaving open." Garrett closed the door. "Unless they've worked their way into the organization and can contribute in other ways, he gets rid of them. My guess is this one's just eighteen—" he looked at the unconscious teenager through the windshield "—or he managed to cross Velasquez somehow."

She supposed that now was the time to share a little information. Before it came to light on its own.

"Your first guess wins." Garrett looked at her sharply. She gestured at the boy. "Let me introduce you to Joe Stafford—Kathy's boyfriend. I saw his picture in his brother's house." She frowned, rethinking the logistics, then glanced over toward where she'd hidden her vehicle. "Maybe we should put him in my car."

The kid was staying right where he was. Garrett wouldn't put it past Megan to try to lose him once the kid was transferred to her car. "Why, because you took a course in EMS?"

If he was thinking of intimidating her with that dark look he was aiming at her, he was going to have to do a whole lot better than that, she thought.

"No, because you might try to lose me now that you know where the transponder is."

The accusation, because it was dead-on, made him smile. "The thought crossed my mind." But he had a bigger problem at the moment than wanting to shake her loose. "But right now, I'm going to have more trouble finding a hospital—"

Megan knew when to grab an opportunity. "No problem. You follow me."

His eyes narrowed dubiously. "You're familiar with the area?"

"Absolutely."

All she needed, Megan thought hurrying away, was enough time to get into her car and look at the map before she turned the vehicle around. Hospitals were clearly indicated on the grid pages, and she always kept maps of all the surrounding states in the trunk of her car.

"I'll pull the car around." She tossed the words over her shoulder as she hurried away. "Wait for me."

He didn't want to, but at the moment he had no other choice.

Megan pulled into an empty space in the hospital's emergency room parking lot less than twenty minutes later. Yanking up the hand brake, she was almost out of the vehicle before it had a chance to come to a full stop. Along the way, she'd had enough time to worry about the consequences if Joe died. Right now, he was her best lead.

She was at the passenger side when Garrett pulled up in the space next to hers. Anxiously, she peered at the boy's face. His eyes were shut, and he looked completely lifeless. She stared at the shallow chest for signs of movement.

"Is he still alive?" she demanded.

"Just barely." Garrett cut the engine. He would rather have called the paramedics to tend to the kid, but grudgingly had to admit that Megan had been right. The extra time it would have taken for them to arrive would probably have cost the boy his life.

Megan had Joe unbuckled by the time Garrett rounded the hood. He easily swept the boy into his arms. "Let's go."

Nodding, she turned and ran ahead, bursting in so quickly that the edges of the electronic doors brushed against her arms before they were fully retracted. Paying no attention, Megan grabbed hold of the first nurse she came across, stopping the woman in her tracks.

Surprised, the nurse instinctively tugged to break Megan's hold on her arm. Megan's hand tightened.

"We've got a teenager who ODed on drugs. He needs treatment—or he's not going to make it. We need a doctor. Now." Authority rang in her voice as she barked out the words.

The nurse only hesitated long enough to look at the boy in Garrett's arms before hurrying off to get the doctor on call.

Garrett could only shake his head. Maybe it was a good thing that for now, Megan had aligned herself with him. "Are you this good about getting a table in a crowded restaurant?"

The question coaxed out half a smile. "Only when I'm starving."

Amused by her answer, he found himself thinking that he wanted to be around when that happened.

Within moments, the nurse returned with a doctor and several other people in her wake, including an official-looking woman holding a clipboard and more than a few papers in her hands.

"We're not sure what he took, but more than likely it's cocaine," Garrett told the doctor.

Smooth-faced, the resident in the white lab coat looked too young to shave. Garrett wondered if he was getting too old for this job, or if it had just prematurely aged him.

"We'll take it from here." The resident turned to

give instructions to the orderlies, who had brought a gurney over with them.

The woman with the clipboard caught their attention. "I'm going to need some information," she informed them, as capable hands took Joe from Garrett and placed the teenager on a gurney. With a penetrating look, she glanced from Garrett to Megan, temporarily withholding judgment. "Which of you is the patient's next of kin?"

"Neither of us," Megan snapped before Garrett had a chance to answer. She hated red tape, even though it seemed to be as much a part of life as breathing. With effort, she softened her tone. "We found him. We're with the DEA." Knowing she probably had less than a second before Wichita challenged her with the truth, Megan turned to him suddenly. "Don't just stand there, Wichita. Show the woman your ID."

More astounded than annoyed, Garrett produced his ID for the administrator, then took over. He had no intention of being run over by an overenergized blonde with a killer body and an even deadlier tongue.

"The boy's a potential witness in an ongoing investigation. We found him less than half an hour ago, and he's apparently been drugged and left to die. I need to question him when he regains consciousness," Garrett emphasized.

Out of the corner of his eye, he saw Megan's face. She looked annoyed about being left out. *Good.*

The hospital administrator pursed her lips uncertainly. "Then the government will be paying for his care?"

Garrett understood the bottom line more than anyone. It always came down to that. Money. "It'll be taken care of."

The woman nodded, though not entirely placated. "As long as you sign for it." She turned a page. "I'll need a name."

Megan interceded, picking up the ball again. "Joe Stafford." It took her only a second to recall Joe's address. "Last known address was 1782 Bigford Road in Bedford, California."

Writing quickly, the administrator filled in the top form, then gave it to Garrett to sign. She looked far from satisfied, but for now she appeared willing to retreat. Tucking the clipboard under her arm, she indicated the swinging blue doors to her left.

"You can stay in the waiting room if you like. I'm sure the doctor will have someone call you if Mr. Stafford regains consciousness."

If.

The word loomed before Megan. It was such a terrible word, creating an almost insurmountable chasm that separated her from Kathy.

Megan tried to bridle her impatience.

"Thank you," Garrett said tersely to the administrator. Taking Megan by the arm, he pushed open the door and forcibly ushered her into the waiting area. "Okay, what's this 'we' business?" he demanded in a low growl.

Uncoupling herself from him with dignity, Megan shrugged carelessly. "I figured it would save time and a lot of useless questions if I let her think we were both with the DEA.''

"Let her?" he echoed incredulously. "You *told* her you were with the DEA."

Tired, Megan sank down on one of the bright orange vinyl sofas. "Don't split hairs. Besides, I figure the federal government has more clout than I do."

He took a seat next to her. Its misshapen cushion shifted, bringing their bodies closer than either of them intended. He felt her tense as her thigh slid against his. Garrett pretended not to notice.

"Nice of you to recognize that. Now maybe you'll also recognize the fact that you're in over your head, and should leave the rest of this to professionals. In case you haven't noticed," he pointed out tersely, "these people play for keeps."

Just who did he think he was—taking that superior tone with her? He was talking to her as if she were some wide-eyed novice. Megan raised her chin, ready to put him in his place.

"I *am* a professional."

"Plunking down a few dollars for a private investigator license, and answering a few simpleminded questions doesn't make you a professional."

She should have insisted Joe be put in her car and then left this fool to find his own way off the hilltop. "Does being with the FBI for four years qualify in your book?" Her voice dripped with sarcasm.

Some of the wind left his sails, though he didn't show it. After a beat, Garrett wasn't sure he believed her claim. "You were an FBI agent?"

She tossed her head. "That's 'Special' agent to you, and yes, I was."

It would be a simple enough thing to check out. "They throw you out?"

"No," Megan bit off. "I left."

"Why?" He waited to shoot her story down.

"Too many rules." Megan stared at him pointedly. "Too many stiff-necked bureaucrats with superior attitudes."

His laugh was soft. And disparaging. "Wouldn't take much to be superior in this case."

She'd had just about enough of this smug agent with his tight butt, magnetic blue eyes...and annoying attitude. Megan crossed her arms before her to keep from strangling him. "I found you, I found the boy, and I found the hospital. Care to reword the last statement?"

"No," he said mildly, infuriating her. "I don't. You were lucky."

He had to say that, she thought. His ego would suffer if he was forced to acknowledge that she was just as capable as he was. "I'd prefer to think of it as skillful."

"Yes, I'm sure you would." Garrett blew out a breath, then reconsidered. Snipping at one another wasn't going to get them anywhere. "Look, I'll admit you've been helpful—"

"Entirely against my will—"

"I figured as much," he cut in. "But since we both have claims to the kid, and you did get to him first, why don't we call a truce?"

"What are you up to?"

He tried to keep his expression impassive. "Not a thing."

The verbal duel was interrupted when the resident with the too-fresh face entered the waiting room. Megan and Garrett were both on their feet by the time he reached them.

"We've stabilized him for now," the doctor said. He looked relieved and pleased—and perhaps, Garrett reevaluated, a little older than fifteen. "You got him here just in time. Another half-hour and he would have been going out in a body bag."

And that, Garrett acknowledged silently, had been Megan's doing. "When can I talk to him?"

The doctor shook his head. "He's still unconscious. There's no telling for how long." He looked from one to the other, his intentions kindly. "I suggest you come back in the morning."

"Not an option," Garrett answered.

"We're here for the duration," Megan put in.

The doctor nodded at the sagging sofa. "Then make yourselves comfortable." He glanced at the oversize clock on the wall. "The cafeteria's still open, but you might be better off with the vending machines down the hall. They have soft drinks and coffee that won't take paint off the side of a house." He was already withdrawing. "I'll let you know if there's any change."

Megan murmured her thanks as she dug into her pocket for change.

Far from satisfied, Garrett looked at her. The outline

of her jeans strained against her body as she rummaged in her pocket. He focused his mind on the immediate problem. "We don't both have to stay, you know."

Her eyes met his. "Yeah, we do. Don't let the hair color fool you, Wichita. I'm not dumb enough to think you'll let me know anything."

He made no comment. He didn't have to. They both knew she was right. He took out a couple of dollars. "Want some coffee?"

She stopped rummaging. "A peace offering? Sure, why not? I've got a cast-iron stomach." She sighed, following him down the hall. The vending machines stood side by side, housed in a small alcove. "It looks like it's going to be a long night."

At least they agreed on something, Garrett thought, slipping the first dollar into the slot.

Chapter 7

"I've found Joe Stafford."

Shifting hands, Megan put the telephone receiver against her other ear and turned in the hall so that her back was to Garrett. She didn't particularly like having an audience while she made her phone call, but he was making no effort to give her any privacy.

The man had a long way to go in brushing up on his social skills, she thought darkly.

On the other end of the line, she heard Judith Teasdale's sharp intake of breath.

"Is Kathy with him? Can I talk to her?"

The hopeful note in the woman's voice made Megan's heart ache—for both Kathy's parents and for Kathy as well. Try as she might to be angry at the girl for making her family go through this, she couldn't summon the emotion. She knew that by now, the girl had more than paid for her rash actions. Megan could feel nothing but pity for the teenager whose picture she carried in her wallet.

"Kathy's not with him, Mrs. Teasdale."

"Where is she? Can't you make him tell you?"

"I wish I could." She sighed, feeling so helpless that she couldn't stand it. "Joe's been in an accident. He was unconscious when we found him," she hurried to add, trying to avoid any questions. "And we've taken him to the hospital."

"We?" Judith asked uncertainly.

"Yes. The DEA agent who came to see you yesterday is here at the hospital with me." Megan could just sense the smile curving along Wichita's lips; she didn't have to look over her shoulder to confirm it. "It seems that our paths crossed again."

"Where is he?" Judith wanted to know, her voice rising. "Where's the monster who made my baby run away? Can I see him?"

"Not easily. He's in Scottsdale. The doctors are working on him now, and he still hasn't come around. Why don't you just let me—"

Suddenly, Warren was on the line as well. She'd had a feeling he couldn't be far from the phone when it rang. They were the kind of people who kept vigils. For them, life had stopped the moment Kathy had slipped out of the house.

"Is that DEA agent looking for Kathy, too?" Megan could hear the barely controlled fear in his voice. "Level with us, Miss Andreini. What kind of danger is our little girl in?"

Megan bit her lower lip. *God help me for lying,* she thought. But right now, in order to stay sane, the Teasdales needed to be lied to.

"No more than any other runaway." She made the answer as sincere-sounding as she could. "There's nothing more to tell you right now. I just wanted you to know where I was and what was happening."

"Yes." The word was tight with unspoken emotions. "Thank you for calling in," Warren murmured.

"Please," Judith begged.

She didn't have to say anymore. Megan understood. "I'll be in touch when I have anything else, Mrs. Teasdale. And I'll find her." It was a promise.

She didn't bother turning around as she plunked in more coins, tapped out a long-distance number and then listened to the metallic recording tell her how much more was needed. There was probably a judgmental look on Wichita's face—or a superior one. In either case, she didn't want to see it.

The added coins made a melodic sound as they rained down through the slot.

The receiver on the other end picked up on the third ring. She waited to see if the greeting came from a human voice or an answering machine.

It was the machine.

She hated talking to machines. Where was her brother? His last class was over, and he had a major paper due. Why wasn't he home, working on it? A tiny shoot of fear pushed through. Megan hoped there was nothing wrong.

"Rusty, it's Megan. I'm in Scottsdale. Don't know

how long I'll be here. Look in on Mom for me tonight, will you? See if she needs anything. You know how she gets.'' Suppressing a sigh that would give away just how weary she felt at the moment, Megan ended the message. ''I'll call you when I can. Oh, and I hope your term paper's going well—which it would be if you were home right now, working on it. Bye.''

Her calls finished, she hung up and turned around. Garrett was watching her, just the way she figured he would be. Actually, it was more like studying her. Or maybe *dissecting* her would be a more accurate description, she thought. Annoyance scrambled up through her on tiny, pointy feet.

''Bossing people around come naturally to you?''

Bone-tired, Megan felt the edges of her temper fraying. ''He was supposed to be home, writing his paper. It's due next Monday.''

Amusement mingled with curiosity. ''How old is he?''

She knew what Wichita was implying. ''Twenty-two. And sometimes, everyone needs to be prodded.'' She spared him an accusing look. ''Don't you have anything better to do than hang around and eavesdrop?''

Leaning against a wall, Garrett straightened as she pushed passed him and headed back to her seat with a container of now-lukewarm coffee.

Turning to follow, he pretended to think, then shook his head. ''None that I can think of.''

Actually, he amended mentally, his eyes drawn to the subtle, unconscious sway of her hips as she walked away from him, that wasn't entirely true. He could think of something a whole lot more satisfying than listening to one side of a conversation. The way he saw it, the crackle of electricity humming between them would have lit up Ben Franklin's heart, not to mention his kite.

Garrett waited until she sat down, then took a seat in the chair adjacent to the sofa. It was easier on him than sitting next to her and having their limbs touch from time to time. "Is Rusty your brother?"

"Why?"

The protective look in her eyes intrigued him. Why did she need to feel so defensive? It seemed an innocent enough question.

Draping his arms over the edges of the chair, Garrett shrugged nonchalantly. "Just passing the time. The magazines are old, and I've already heard the news three times."

To underscore his point, he indicated with his eyes the mounted television set over in the corner. The channel was set to a local all-news station that, while entertaining at first, had gotten irritatingly repetitive. It was a slow news evening.

Megan paused before answering, as if weighing the wisdom of saying anything remotely personal to this man. The coffee was worse than lukewarm: it was cold. And bad. She drank it anyway, needing the caffeine.

"Yes, Rusty's my brother."

Maybe it was just his intrusion she resented, rather than something she felt that she had to guard, Garrett guessed. Nodding at the scrap of information, he looked out the window.

Everything seemed dead outside, blanketed in darkness so that he was only able to see out a few feet. Inside, they were the only two people in the waiting area. Apparently the news wasn't the only thing that was slow tonight. The ER was as empty as a tomb.

He looked in her direction again. What made a woman like her tick? One minute she was sexy; the next, stand-offish. And all the while, there was this go-to-hell independence that throbbed just beneath.

And what was beneath that? he wondered.

"Got any other siblings?"

Why all these questions? Megan wondered. "Another brother." Her eyes locked with his. If he could ask, so could she. "You?"

"No."

He said it with such finality that she felt chills along her spine. His tone posted a ten-foot sign in front of him, warning off trespassers. But if that's what he wanted, he shouldn't have asked *her* any questions.

"Only child?" She watched his expression, waiting for a response.

His face betrayed nothing. "Yeah. Now."

For a charmer, he'd suddenly become as communicative as a tree.

All right, Megan thought. She could respect privacy, even if she couldn't. For now, she left his personal life alone.

Restless, she got up and threw away the empty paper container in the trash, then looked accusingly at the double doors that led into the ER treatment room. The doctor hadn't come out to see them since he'd initially talked to them more than two hours ago. She stared, willing the doors to open.

Nothing.

"What's keeping him?"

Waiting was all part of the game to Garrett. He'd schooled himself to be patient. "Probably has nothing to say." He toyed with the idea of asking his next question, then decided to go ahead. "Why did you lie to them?"

The question came out of nowhere. Megan turned around to look at him. "Who?"

Garrett pointed in the general direction of the telephones. "The Teasdales. It wasn't hard making out their side of the conversation. Why didn't you tell them that Stafford ODed on drugs that had probably been pumped into him? Why tell them the kid was in an accident?"

He probably wouldn't understand, but she told him anyway. "Because they're a nice couple, heretofore living a nice life. They're not made to handle things like drugs and dealers and overdosing. I don't want to make them worry any more than they already are."

Garret shook his head and laughed. She thought he was laughing at her, until he said, "'Heretofore'? Who the hell says 'heretofore'?"

"I do," she answered crisply. Her eyes narrowed as she pinned him to his chair. "Some of us like building our communication skills instead of just grunting like primal creatures."

"I strike you as a primal creature?" The thought amused him. It was not without its own implications.

Megan nodded. "Just barely upright." Her mouth quirked as she tried to suppress a smile. Then she laughed softly, shaking her head when he looked at her quizzically. "Must be the pace," she decided. "I feel like I'm getting giddy."

Leaning back in the chair, his eyes swept over her face. "Whatever it is, you look better when you smile." When unguarded, there was a sweet innocence to her smile that he knew she wouldn't appreciate his mentioning.

Getting to his feet, he started toward the vending machines again. There was nothing else to do right now. "Want another cup of coffee?"

"Only if I want to gain access to the ER from the other side and have my stomach pumped," Megan said, following him. "That was foul."

"Yeah, it was," he agreed amiably. Garrett pulled out a handful of change from his pocket. The bills he had left were all larger denominations than the machine was prepared to take. "I can spring for a candy bar." He had just enough for two. "How about it?"

Instead of answering, she pointed to a selection, then glanced at him, as if suspecting a motive. "Why are you being so nice?"

He fed the machine, then pressed the numbers indicated beneath the selection.

"Just my true nature." A curled metal rod pushed out a candy bar filled with peanuts, then withdrew. The candy bar plunged to the bottom of the machine and waited to be rescued. Garrett pushed aside the glass, plucked it out, then offered it to Megan. "Why are you being so suspicious?"

With a nod of thanks, she took the candy bar from him. "Because I spent a lot of time around government agents and their 'real' true nature."

He fed more coins into the machine and made a second selection. Nothing happened. "Which is?"

He tapped the numbers out again, but the candy remained where it was. "Do anything you have to in order to bring the case to a close." Elbowing him aside, she positioned her hand at an angle, then struck the front of the machine with it. The coil around the candy bar retracted, and the candy fell. "That means lie, twist things and ignore people in your way."

He fished out his dinner, then tore open one side. The woman was definitely handy to have around. "Sounds cold."

"It is. And you know it." Megan led the way back to the waiting room. The doctor was nowhere in sight. Resigned, she looked at Garrett. "Tell me what else you know."

He tore back a little more of the wrapper, then bit into the chewy offering. "Alphabetically or chronologically?"

"Just about Kathy," she said, not sounding as annoyed as she had earlier.

There, he could afford to be honest with her. "You have the sum total already. I saw her on the surveillance tape, ran her face through the files on the various web sites for missing kids, and came up with a match.'' He didn't bother sitting down. ''Any lead in a storm.''

''She's not a lead—she's a young, innocent girl.''

Finishing the candy bar, Garrett crumpled the blue-and-gold wrapper and then tossed it toward the wastepaper container. The wrapper went in. Only then did he look at Megan.

''Yeah, I know.''

Something in his voice made Megan look at him. Maybe it was the hour, or maybe she really was getting giddy and lax, but she believed him. At least about this.

Finished eating, she absently folded the wrapper in half, then in half again. ''What are her chances of staying innocent?''

Garrett had already decided that Megan was more savvy than she first appeared. Maybe a lot more savvy.

''You know the answer to that better than I do. Slimmer every day.'' And that was the real tragedy of it. ''Forget about innocent, just concentrate on finding her alive.''

Megan raised an eyebrow. ''Advice from the competition?''

He heard a touch of amusement in her voice and didn't know just why he found it so attractive. Garrett shoved his hands into his pockets and shrugged. ''Take it while it's free.''

''There is no such thing as free.'' Everything, Megan knew, came with a price. What price did he want to exact from her?

Just when Garrett thought he had her pegged, she

changed direction on him again. He studied her for a long moment. "That's pretty cynical, even for a former government agent." A half smile played on his lips. "Born that way?"

No, she hadn't been born that way. She'd been born an optimist. Until she'd been taught otherwise. "Circumstances."

And suddenly, Garrett realized he wanted to know about those circumstances. He told himself that it was because he always wanted to know everything there was about a case. But he didn't know if he actually believed himself. "Care to elaborate?"

Megan set her mouth hard. "No."

He looked at her for a long moment. He wasn't about to coax it out of her, if that was what she was waiting for. But he did want to know.

"It's going to be a long night," he said mildly, "and I didn't bring any cards."

It was on the tip of Megan's tongue to demand to know what that had to do with anything.

That was why she had absolutely no idea what it was that made her give him an answer. Maybe she just needed someone to talk to to fill the minutes that were dragging by. Or maybe she knew that if Wichita really wanted to know about any part of her background, he could pull a few strings and get his hands on her file.

Just as easily as she could get her hands on his.

More easily, in fact.

She folded her hands in front of her, looking down at her fingertips. "My brother was kidnapped when I was a kid."

Suddenly, Garrett understood. "Did they ever find him?"

She raised her head. The eyes that met his were angry. Very angry.

"Yeah, they found him," Megan said bitterly. "But not before my mother had had a complete nervous breakdown. Not before my other brother and I became prisoners of nightmares that refused to go away." *Even years later.*

There were times when she still woke up in a cold sweat, dreaming that some unseen hand had come to snatch her away from home, the way it had Chad.

Garrett heard what he felt was the only important thing. "If they found him, then your brother was one of the lucky ones."

"I know that," she snapped at him. There was no reason to cry, not after all these years. It was all done with and in the past. Megan felt moisture along her lashes anyway. She looked away. "They found Chad with my father two-and-a-half years after he'd been kidnapped." Like a robot incapable of feeling, she recited, "Two-and-a-half years after my father swore he had nothing to do with it. Two-and-a-half years after he supposedly flew in from Houston to hold my mother's hand and comfort her when the ordeal started."

Garrett saw the raw emotion in her eyes when she looked at him again.

"My father served six months in prison, then his lawyer got the verdict overturned on some technicality. As far as I know, he's going on very well with his life.''

Megan hadn't seen her father in all these years. Not even once. She couldn't bring herself to do so. Not after what he'd done to everyone.

Not after he'd killed everything within her that could trust someone.

"And your mother?'' Garrett asked softly.

"Finding Chad helped bring her around, but she's never been the same since.''

There was no point in saying anything about the depths of depression her mother had sunk to, or the hospital confinements over the years. Or how Megan had had to be the mother to both her own mother and to Rusty even before she saw her teens.

"Chad went into law enforcement.'' It was the only way, she knew, that Chad could make peace with the world around him. And with his own life.

Garrett was far more interested in her motives. "Is that why you did, too?''

Megan answered before she realized that Wichita was drawing out bits of her. "I did it so that maybe I could help spare someone from going through the hell my mother did.''

He took her hand, forcing her to look at him. "How about the hell you went through?''

It was a surprisingly sensitive question—for a government agent. Her mouth curved.

"Maybe you're not as thick-skinned as I thought. Most people don't realize that the victim's siblings hurt just as much as the parents do.'' Belatedly, she realized he was holding her hand. She drew it away. "Maybe more—because they're afraid it'll happen to them, too."

"And worse if they find out that someone they idolized is responsible."

She looked at him sharply. He had no right to probe her like this. "I never said I idolized my father."

"Yes, you did. Just not out loud."

Her defense shields slid back into place. "Practicing Psych 101?"

Garrett shrugged at the sarcastic tone, knowing its source was pain. "Comes in handy at times."

It was too late to tell him to back off, Megan thought. He'd already delved too deeply. But if he'd made her expose herself to him, the least he could do was return the favor.

Megan tossed her hair over her shoulder. "Okay, we've played true confession with my life. What's your story?"

Garrett had no intention of going there. "I don't have a story."

His reaction was just what Megan would have anticipated. But she wasn't going to give up. "Everyone has a story."

"Mine's just a footnote." Because Garrett knew she wouldn't back off, he gave her just the barest of scraps. "I want to get slime like Velasquez away from people like Kathy and that kid on the gurney."

"That's very altruistic-sounding. Did you just one day wake up and decide to pick up the mantle of the Masked Avenger, or is there something more to it than that?'' When he didn't say anything, Megan felt she had her answer, at least in part. ''Does it have something to do with your saying that you're an only child now?''

His admission about that had just come out. And it shouldn't have. Annoyed, Garrett snapped, ''Let's just drop it, all right?''

''Not after you just went kibitzing through my guts, we don't.'' She saw his frown and ignored it. ''Okay, let me take a stab at this. Velasquez sold drugs to your sister or brother or whoever, and you're looking for revenge. Am I close?''

''Not close, just annoying.'' He got up, terminating the conversation.

It felt like a slap in the face, but Megan recovered. There was no way she'd give him the satisfaction of knowing. She shrugged indifferently. ''Have it your way.''

''I intend to,'' he said, walking away from her.

She watched his back. It was stiff, as if someone had just shoved a rod between his shoulder blades.

''If you keep stuff like that inside you long enough,'' she called after him, ''it'll eat you alive.''

He stopped and then turned around. ''Now who's practicing Psych 101?''

''I never practice anything.'' She grinned. ''I just do it.''

He had no doubt about that.

Chapter 8

Megan didn't remember falling asleep. She didn't even realize that her eyes had closed until the muted sounds of a small child's crying invaded her subconscious and made her jolt.

Her eyes flew open in embarrassment.

Coming around, she looked at the clock on the wall, which was easier to focus on at the moment than the watch on her wrist.

Megan blew out a breath, annoyed. Somehow, it had gotten to be seven in the morning without her fully realizing how. The last time she'd looked, it had been almost four. That meant she'd lost about three hours somewhere.

Her mouth had a sticky, sweet taste in it. The chocolate bar, she thought. That, too, was going to remain with her for a while.

The last thing she remembered was talking to Wichita about Houston.

Wichita.

The name shot through her brain like a bullet, just a microsecond before she realized that he was no longer sitting opposite her. Or anywhere in the immediate vicinity.

Shooting to her feet, she felt something drop from her lap. She hadn't even realized there was something there. Megan bent down to pick it up, her back protesting. Her fingers closed around the small transponder she'd inserted in Wichita's trunk.

Heaping silent curses on his absent head, Megan quickly crossed to the registration desk. There were new faces on the other side of the barrier. The night shift was gone. One woman was busy taking information from the distraught young mother of the crying child.

Agitation strummed through her as Megan turned to the clerk in the next cubicle. "Do you know where the man who was sitting with me went?"

The woman looked at her blankly.

She should have known better, Megan thought. "Never mind."

Turning abruptly, she hurried to the stationary doors she'd been watching half the night. Behind her, she heard a chair being scraped along the floor as it was pushed back.

"You can't go in there," the woman called after her.

Watch me, Megan thought. Everything, apparently, had gone wrong.

She rushed into the treatment area to see the ER physician walking to the rear exit. Beyond lay the emergency parking lot.

"Wait!" Reaching him in time, Megan grabbed the resident's arm to keep him from leaving. "You never got back to me."

He looked at her, puzzled and just a little wary of her erratic behavior.

"Yes, I did. I came out when the patient regained consciousness."

"When was that?" She realized that the question came out like a demand, but being double-crossed rarely brought out the best in her.

The physician thought a moment. "Around five." He didn't see what was wrong. "The other agent said there was no sense in waking you up, too. That he would handle it."

She just bet he did. Five. That meant Wichita had more than a two-hour headstart. He could be anywhere. She had to talk to Joe.

"Where's Stafford now?"

"He's in ICU. Stable, but guarded."

"Where's—?"

He anticipated her question. "Down the hall past the elevators to your left."

Megan nodded, finally releasing her hold on the resident's arm. For his benefit, she attempted half a smile. "Thank you."

She glanced out into the lot as the resident hurried

away through the doors, obviously glad to put the night, and her, behind him.

Wichita's car was gone. What a surprise.

With some fast talking, Megan managed to get past the receptionist in the intensive care unit.

At first glance, Joe Stafford looked even worse than he had when Megan first discovered him. The only difference was that some of his color had returned.

Megan gently placed a hand on Joe Stafford's shoulder and roused him.

The brown eyes that finally opened and looked up at her were hazy and blank.

Megan wasn't even sure if they were focused. "Joe, can you hear me?"

"Yeah…" Each word sounded as if it came from a long distance away. "Do I know…you?"

"No." She shook her head and forced an encouraging smile, telling herself not to dwell on the harm Stafford had done. It wouldn't help. "But you know Kathy. Where did they take her?"

"Kathy?" The name seemed to mean nothing to him. The blank stare deepened until it seemed to take over his entire face.

"Kathy Teasdale," she said slowly, waiting for the name to register. "Kathy—the girl you ran off with." Still nothing. "Short, blonde, fourteen."

Megan struggled to control her temper. If not for this misguided, poor excuse for a human being, Kathy would be home with her family, looking forward to all the things a fourteen-year-old girl was entitled to.

"Your girlfriend."

A faint light entered his eyes as something finally clicked into place. With effort, he tried to move his head from side to side, but succeeded only in a slight twitch. "I dunno...a trip...they sent me...on my own...trip."

There wasn't time for this. Megan lowered her face to his ear. "A trip to where?"

"Hands...something...no...palms...maybe."

Megan stared at him. She had no clue what he was trying to say, and he was beginning to drift away again. And then a thought came to her from nowhere. Velasquez went where the rich went.

"Palm Springs? Did they take her to Palm Springs?"

A labored breath found its way into his lungs. "Yeah...maybe."

Megan saw the nurse approaching her. There wasn't time for more questions.

Garrett felt rather pleased as he embarked on the last leg of his trip to Palm Springs. The road was clear, he was making good time, and the temperatures were mild for this time of year. He should be in the heart of the city in less than an hour.

The DEA's connections had yielded the name and address of Velasquez's main contact in the city, based on the fragmented ramblings of a kid in the hospital. From where he stood, that was a pretty fair accomplishment.

He had a lot to feel good about. Word on the street was that Velasquez was here to meet with a supplier.

Though the particulars were still hazy, the pieces looked as if they were finally falling into place. And if that wasn't enough, he'd managed to sneak off and lose Megan.

Right about now, he figured he was feeling as good as he was ever going to.

The smile on his lips faded a little.

Triumph wasn't quite as high a feeling as it should have been. But that would undoubtedly come, he promised himself and the memory of his brother, once he had Velasquez behind bars.

Little by little, Garrett's thoughts strayed back to Megan. He wondered how she'd reacted, waking up in the ER waiting room to find that he was gone. Probably madder than a wet hen, and spewing words that would make truck drivers blush.

The notion made him grin to himself. Megan Andreini was some piece of work.

He had to admit that he'd never met a woman quite like Megan before—one who caught his fancy this way. A woman he thought of as his equal.

A woman who lingered on in his mind once their moment together was gone.

Realizing as much made him feel uneasy. This was something new, something he couldn't prepare for, couldn't train for. And strapping on a gun wouldn't help.

He didn't like being unarmed.

Garrett shook himself free of the thought. He didn't have time to dwell on her, he reminded himself. It would only gum things up, and he needed a clear mind for what was ahead.

But the road continued to stretch before him, and thoughts of Megan continued to sneak back into his mind. Almost against his will, he thought back to the last conversation they'd had just before her eyes had closed and she'd surrendered to sleep.

It came back to him almost verbatim.

"You're from Houston?" he'd asked in surprise and suspicion when she'd volunteered that small tidbit to him around three-thirty. There'd been some old black-and-white movie with stilted dialogue and fake scenery on the television, making Megan seem all the more vivid.

There'd been mischief in her eyes as she'd answered. "Just because I don't drawl and my mouth isn't filled with warm honey when I talk doesn't mean I can't be from your hometown."

But her mouth *had* tasted like warm honey when he'd kissed her, Garrett remembered thinking. Actually, more like hot honey that swirled and oozed all through him the moment his lips had touched hers.

"You don't believe me," she'd guessed when he'd said nothing in reply.

He'd shrugged then, thinking that she would probably say anything to give them common ground, hoping to maybe disarm him that way. As if he could so easily be misled.

He'd narrowed his eyes and just looked at her, but she hadn't squirmed. "Should I?"

"I don't really care if you do or not." And then,

because he supposed it wasn't in her nature to back off from anything—even something as simple as a challenge in a conversation exchanged in an empty hospital waiting room—she'd gone on to add, ''I was born in St. Augustine Hospital.''

An eerie feeling had undulated through him, and it took effort on his part to ignore it. She'd probably had a chance to pull up his file somehow. He wouldn't have put it past her. Wouldn't have, he'd realized, put anything past this woman. She was as devious as they came.

''So was I.''

He'd watched her eyes when he said it, and saw surprise and disbelief enter. It almost convinced him that she was on the level. Either that, or one hell of a fine actress.

She'd moved to the edge of her seat then, peering into his eyes and making him think about things that had nothing to do with keeping an endless vigil in a antiseptic-smelling room.

''I lived at 18 Shorter Road.''

He was more than familiar with the street. By then he was certain that she was putting him on. This was far too much of a coincidence.

''I lived about a mile from there.'' At least he had until the accident that had turned Andy and him into orphans. ''3781 Harper.''

Her eyes had narrowed then to glints of enticing green that had temporarily mesmerized him. ''No, you didn't.''

If Garrett hadn't known better, he would have said

that he was the one trying to fool her instead of the other way around.

"Yeah, I did. And I went to—" It had taken him a minute to remember. "P.S. 11."

Megan shook her head at the mention of the public elementary school. "We left before I ever got to go to school."

She'd contemplated her fingertips then, as if relating the story—even in vague fragments—was hard for her. He imagined that it was her way of reeling him in, but it seemed so genuine that for the space of a few minutes, he found himself believing her.

"We moved around a bit for a few years, never staying more than a year in one place—usually less. My father could never hold down anything for very long. It was always someone else's fault why he quit." And from the look that passed over her face when she said it, Garrett knew that she'd believed her father, and believed *in* him, with all her young heart. "And then my mother took my brothers and me to live near her mother in Southern California."

She'd said it as if it were a throwaway line, and he knew that it wasn't. And that whatever else had come before, this was the truth. "Parents divorced?"

"Separated. Legally," she added after a beat. "My mother didn't believe in divorce." Megan shrugged, as if creating a barrier between herself and what she was saying. As if anything else still hurt too much. "She'd said that she never intended to marry anyone else, so there was no need for an official divorce. For the first two years after that, I kept hoping they'd get together…''

She shrugged again—a little half shrug that was the only evidence of self-consciousness he'd seen from her. She'd looked up at him accusingly.

''What did you put in that coffee you gave me? I've talked more to you than…'' Her voice trailed off and she waved away the rest of her statement, leaving him to wonder about it then.

And now.

Had there been someone else she'd talked to, someone else she'd opened up her wounds to? Probably. And it shouldn't have mattered in the slightest to him if there had been. But it still did.

She'd lapsed into silence after that, and he let it continue, feeling that he already knew more about her than he should have. The more he knew, the more his thoughts could stray, and he wanted no reason for her to be more than a passing thought in his mind.

It looked as if he didn't have much say in that, Garrett thought now, frowning. She was there, in every thought, like a clear layer of varnish that coated a fine piece of furniture. You couldn't really see it, but it made its presence known.

It didn't matter, Garrett told himself. He wasn't going to see her again. Not if things laid themselves out the way he hoped they would.

An hour later, Garrett had staked out a table at a trendy coffee shop located near one of the four corners of Chapman and Main. From where he sat, he could see clearly the Mexican take-out place and the street in front of it. His informant was supposed to walk by at approximately two-thirty. Having arrived early, Garrett was nursing a cup of coffee that boasted three names. He sipped, but hardly tasted it.

He turned the pages of the newspaper propped up in front of him just often enough to make it appear that he was reading. Behind his tinted sunglasses, his eyes never wavered from the street scene outside.

Everyone who drove by was suspect. There was very little foot traffic. He was counting on that.

Garrett brought the rim of the cup to his lips, and then froze. The cup came down hard against the saucer, sloshing the hot liquid over the sides. His mouth hardened as a feeling of déjà vu came over him.

What the hell was she doing here?

Peeling off a five and tossing it on the emerald-green tablecloth, Garrett quickly rose to his feet and strode out of the restaurant.

Behind him, he heard the waitress calling out. "Is anything wrong with the coffee?" He ignored her. There was no time for niceties. He had the uneasy feeling that everything was going to blow up on him.

Why couldn't this woman stay put and keep her nose out of his business?

With his eyes riveted on his target, Garrett crossed the large intersection, paying only marginal attention to the traffic. He was fighting an overwhelming urge to wrap his hands around her long, lovely neck.

Megan, wearing a skirt that looked as if it had been painted on with tiny brush strokes, had one arm looped through the arm of the man he'd been waiting for. If he didn't know any better, he would have said she looked like one of the strolling hostesses of the evening. She'd undoubtedly dressed like this to attract the other man's attention. But how had she known about him in the first place?

Megan looked up a moment before Garrett reached them, a complacent smile on her lips. There seemed to be absolutely no sign of recognition in her eyes when she turned them on him.

"Do you know him?" she whispered to the small man she was with.

Reed thin, with a face that bore silent testimony to a turbulent life, the dark-haired man looked blankly at Garrett. He shrugged indifferently, intent on turning on charm that he didn't realize he didn't have. "I do not think so."

His hand closing around Megan's other arm, Garrett yanked her to his side. "What are you doing here?" he demanded in a low growl against her ear.

She tried to pull away, but knew she couldn't without drawing attention to them. So she looked up at his face and smiled, knowing it would infuriate him.

"Making up for time I lost," she said glibly. "Someone forgot to wake me up this morning."

Clearly bewildered, the man on her other side frowned. "You know him, lady?"

She touched the tip of her tongue to her teeth, as if debating whether or not to deny any knowledge of Garrett. She never got the chance.

With a hand on each of their arms, Garrett pulled

both the wiry informant and Megan over to the side street. "My car's over here." He indicated the sedan.

The informant looked at the vehicle distastefully. It was clearly not the kind of vehicle he favored. "Don't pay you much, do they?"

"It's a rental," Garrett snarled, not bothering to look at Megan. He'd already had this conversation with her. "Get in," he ordered the informant.

Still staring at the car, the man hesitated. He looked at Garrett dubiously. "You got the money?"

"If he doesn't, I do," Megan interjected.

Shooting Megan a dark look, he lamented the fact that justifiable homicide carried such a heavy burden of proof with it, but even so, it was beginning to seem worth the effort.

"I've got the money," he assured the informant. "Now get in the damn car."

To his annoyance, the man got in the back seat. And Megan followed suit.

He'd just about had his fill of her surprises, but something told him she had more in store.

Chapter 9

There was an end to his patience, and Garrett felt that he had reached it three minutes ago. Glaring at Megan, he threw open the front passenger door. "Get in the front seat, Megan."

She sat just where she was, holding her ground. Her face was maddeningly impassive as she looked at him. "You can't order me around."

"Get in the front seat, Megan," Garrett growled again, then tacked on "please" when she still made no effort to move.

"Better," she murmured with a nod, then got in the front.

He slammed the door, then rounded the hood to his side. "Don't push it," he warned under his breath.

Getting in, he spared only a cursory glance around

before he drove the car in reverse, coming out the opposite end of the side street.

"How did you get here?" he wanted to know. "I found your blasted transponder."

Wary of a second plant that she might have conveniently neglected to mention, Garrett had checked the car over thoroughly inside and out before continuing on to Palm Springs. There hadn't been anything. She was a small-time private investigator, tied to a three-man agency. How did she come up with the same information that took a good deal of the DEA workforce to gain?

The leap from the house in Scottsdale to Palm Springs was a large one. Even larger was the one to locating a man he only knew as Skinny Jake. Was there a leak in the department that hadn't been plugged yet?

Megan took her time in answering. Though the situation was dire, she had to admit that she did enjoy pitting her mind against his. If she gave it any thought, Megan couldn't remember when she'd enjoyed a challenge more.

"I went back to the hillside house," she said simply. "Got there just before your people did."

It had been tricky, getting out again without being noticed. There had been at least twenty DEA agents swarming the area, all easily identifiable by the insignias on the backs of their jackets.

"The department has nice taste in jackets, by the way," she added before he had a chance to deny their presence. If he wanted to play games, that was fine with her. As long as she won.

"That still doesn't answer my question."

Some things in life, she thought, like the man sitting next to her, were complicated beyond understanding. Others were exceedingly simple. This had been simple.

Megan smiled at Garrett, unable to resist looking smug. "I pressed the redial button on the telephone in the kitchen. It had an LCD screen. I copied down the number."

The pleasure she derived from seeing Wichita's mouth drop open was incredible. Turning in her seat, she glanced at the painfully thin man sitting behind her. "I traced the number through a reverse phone book. It identified the party's name and led me right to him. After that, I caught a commuter flight."

Surprise immediately melted into concern. Garrett smelled a double-cross. Pulling the car sharply into a nursery parking lot, he turned around to look at the informant's weather-beaten face. Skinny Jake's expression was nothing short of brazen, but that carried no weight with Garrett. He'd spent most of his life trying to brazen things out.

Garrett pinned Jake with a warning look that said he wasn't about to put up with lies. "Why would Velasquez be calling you?"

The laugh rising out of the shallow lungs was more of a dry cackle.

"Not Velasquez, man. Jaime, his nephew. The kid's got the hots for my daughter, Angela. He called her yesterday. Said he was coming back. Told her where he'd be staying and where to meet him.'' Crossing arms that looked far too thin to bear the tattoos that covered them, he grinned broadly at Garrett. ''There's nothing like true love, man.''

Garrett had no idea that the informant even had a family, much less a daughter. The whole story sounded fishy. He had the uneasy feeling that he was being set up.

''And she told you?''

Contempt entered the dark brown eyes that told Garrett that if he believed that, then his brain was smaller than a chickpea.

''No, man, don't you know anything? I *overheard* them,'' he emphasized as if that put him on the same footing as an international spy. He sank down a little in his seat, suddenly realizing whose car he was in. ''Now, maybe you two want to go on hearing yourselves talk, but me, I have to think about my reputation and my health. I ain't gonna have either if I get caught with you.'' He looked leeringly over toward Megan. ''No offense, lady.''

Megan grinned at the odd apology. ''None taken.''

The man's head bobbed up and down like an old-fashioned toy on the dashboard of a vintage car. ''Okay, so you want this information or not?'' The question was shot at Garrett.

Part of Garrett was truly skeptical that what he was paying for would prove to be valid, and he was still wary of a setup. But right now, there were no other leads. Garrett had no choice, and he knew it. He hated not having choices. "I want this information."

If Jake was worried, he gave no indication. From the depths of the back seat a smile flashed, made brighter by contrast with his dark skin. "Good. Now about my price—"

Garrett's eye met his in the rearview mirror. *They always try,* he thought wearily. "That's already been negotiated."

Still watching in the mirror, Garrett saw the brown eyes shift toward Megan. He felt something tightening inside his gut that could easily have been mistaken for rage, if he didn't know better.

"That was before there was someone else in the game. She wants it, too." And the name of the game was clearly money. "Which of you is it going to be? I got no pride, I go to the highest bidder."

Amused, Megan turned to look at Garrett. For half an instant, she thought she saw murder in the DEA agent's eyes. It hit her then that he was probably more than capable of it. She wasn't certain how to fit that realization into the scheme of things.

Twisting in her seat, she looked over her shoulder at Jake. "That's okay, give it to him. He knew you ahead of me."

Garrett lamented the fact that unlike cars in high-tech spy thrillers, his didn't come with an ejection button.

It *did* occur to him that he could sharply turn a corner, and push her out. Tempting though the thought was, he knew he couldn't do it—not in good conscience at any rate.

It was a hell of a time to realize he had one.

Skinny Jake looked disappointed to be reduced to only one customer. He attempted to quibble a little longer, but the threat of being turned in to his own people as an informant quickly terminated all bartering on his part. Jake accepted the initial price he'd agreed to, and, amid obscenities, told them where Velasquez and his entourage were staying.

It was another pricey address. Garrett had expected as much.

With the exchange complete, Garrett and Megan parted company with Jake, leaving the informant in another, less-traveled location.

Megan settled back in her seat, pulling down the edge of her skirt. It kept creeping up on her thigh of its own volition.

"How does he keep getting these houses?" she asked Garrett.

His eyes were drawn to her hand as she tugged on her skirt. Drawn to her hand and the area she was attempting to cover. Anyway you looked at it, the woman had great legs, he thought. He wondered if she was doing that to distract him. It annoyed him that she was succeeding so easily.

"A good real estate agent," he quipped. "That's the least of my questions."

Megan had caught the look in his eyes and felt oddly flattered, though she told herself that it didn't matter one way or another.

"And the most of your questions...?" she teased.

What Garrett perceived as his weakness gave way to annoyance—at himself as well as at her. "Would be why you keep popping up like a slice of toast."

"No one's ever described me as a slice of bread before," Megan said, laughing.

Garrett kept one eye on his rearview mirror, watching for a possible tail. He'd come too far to be complacent now.

"No, I don't imagine they have. Pain in the butt would probably be more accurate." Sparing her a glance as he took a corner, Garrett pressed his lips together. It wasn't easy keeping his temper under wraps with her, but he couldn't afford to let it go—for any of their sakes. "You can't keep doing this."

"I'll stop as soon as I find Kathy." He glared at her. "Just doing my job, Wichita. Just like you," she added evenly.

Stopped at a light, he looked at her. "Mine's a little larger in scope than yours."

Megan didn't see it that way. "Oh, I don't know. A human life is pretty large in scope from where I'm sitting." And she still had a strong feeling that it was the forfeit of a single human life that had initially led him on his crusade. Banking on that was her strongest angle.

The light changed, and Garrett pressed on the accelerator again. Megan shifted in her seat. "Look, I'm not about to give up, and neither are you. So why don't we do what I suggested at the hotel?"

Mention of the hotel brought a whole barrage of

thoughts to him—most unwelcome because of the feelings they created.

"Which was?"

"That we throw in together." She anticipated his reaction and tried to head it off before they engaged in verbal combat again. "I'm only interested in finding Kathy as soon as possible. If putting Velasquez behind bars is the best way, then hey, count me in. I'll do whatever I have to to help you."

Thought a lot of herself, didn't she? Garrett mused. Didn't she realize yet how dangerous all this was? That she could easily wind up hurt—or dead?

"What makes you think I want, or even—laughably—need your help?"

Megan knew he was just trying to aggravate her so that she would back off. Apparently the man had absolutely no clue how stubborn she could be.

"You haven't caught him yet, have you?" she reminded him mildly. "Way I figure it, maybe you need a fresh angle. A man can always use a little more help."

Her eyes were laughing at him, and Garrett knew it should have really ticked him off. Why the sight warmed him instead was completely beyond his comprehension. Maybe he'd spent too long in the field and was beginning to forget which end was up.

He trained his eyes on the road. "Ever hear the one about too many cooks spoiling the broth?"

"I'll keep out of your kitchen," she promised complacently, then slanted a look in his direction, "but not out of your operation."

At this point, he wouldn't have believed her even if she'd promised to turn around and go home. "I could have you arrested."

Megan knew her rights, not to mention the inner workings of most departments. "Not easily."

She looked at his profile, determined now to put this one-upmanship on hold. There were more important things at stake.

"How about it? The alternative is to keep wasting time trying to ditch me. And constantly looking over your shoulder because you know I'm going to 'pop up,' as you put it, again."

She had a point. Garrett didn't like it. Didn't like being backed into a corner. But he knew she was right. And, grudgingly, he had to admit the woman had style and ability. The fact that there was also this under-current of electricity running through him, this grow-ing desire to find out just what the lady was made of, and if she felt as soft in an intimate setting as she was tough on the job, tipped the scales in her favor.

Maybe it shouldn't have, but he was beyond that now. He had the operation to think of.

Garrett waited a beat longer, to give the impression that he was thinking about it further. "If I say yes, we play by my rules."

She raised both hands to shoulder level in a sign of surrender.

"You can have the whole game board." Megan dropped her hands in her lap again. "All I want is one pawn."

So she kept saying. God, he hoped he wasn't going

to regret this. The engine of his car began to whine a little as the vehicle started to climb to a higher altitude. "I'll try to make sure you get it."

She didn't like the qualifying word, and wouldn't go along with it by keeping silent. "Don't 'try.' Do it."

He shifted the vehicle to another gear. "You always been this demanding?"

His tone told her he was giving in, even if he didn't say it. "Ever since the day I was born, they tell me."

Garrett frowned. But not deeply. "I had a feeling."

She laughed for the first time since he'd seen her walking with Jake. He had to admit that there was something about the sound that went right through him, nestling down into parts of him that he had long since thought abandoned.

"Partners?" Megan stuck out her hand.

Stopped at a light, he glanced at it. "Don't get carried away."

With one eye on the traffic light, she took his hand, shook it, then dropped it. "Don't worry, Wichita. I won't get carried away. I know exactly where I stand with you."

That, he figured as the light turned green again, put her one up on him.

Garrett saw the dead man first, and tried to shield Megan, grabbing her by the shoulders and turning her away before she had a chance to enter the room.

Megan's heart stopped in her throat, then beat wildly as she came to the first logical conclusion. "Is it Kathy?'' As she demanded the answer, she broke away from him.

She came to an abrupt stop less than two feet away. Her stomach lurched at the sight of the pool of blood staining the white rug. It framed the dead man's body like a ghoulish outline.

It took her a moment to find her voice. She felt Garrett beside her.

''Velasquez is going to have to start looking around for another color to decorate with, or learn how to hold his temper.'' *At least it wasn't Kathy,* she thought. ''Know who he is?''

Garrett knew, by face and reputation, most of the people inside Velasquez's inner circle. The baby-faced kid had only been part of it for less than a year. His death bore testimony to how heartless Velasquez actually was.

''Yeah. Jaime Caldron.''

She knew the name and stared incredulously at the man's face. ''Velasquez's nephew?''

Crouching beside the body, Garrett looked for signs of life, knowing there weren't any. This job was meant to be thorough. It was a warning.

''Yeah, his nephew. Guess Jaime won't be keeping his rendezvous with Skinny's daughter.'' Disgusted, he dragged his hand through his hair as he rose again. ''Velasquez must have found out that Jaime made that call.''

''And he killed him?'' She knew all about men like that. But even coming face-to-face with evidence, it was still difficult to fathom.

After all this time, Garrett knew exactly how the other man thought. "The organization's more important than anyone except for Velasquez himself. Jaime was careless. He put it all in jeopardy because he let another part of his anatomy do the thinking for him. Velasquez was never known for his forgiveness and understanding."

She nodded. So here they were at another dead end. Literally. Megan stifled a shiver and looked at Garrett. "Now what?"

For just a moment, frustration got the better of him. Two leads gone in almost as many days. It was as if he were being toyed with. Because Megan was standing next to him, he swallowed the barrage of curses that popped so readily into his mouth. His one last hold on polite society, he supposed. And his last link to his very religious parents. Garrett buried the thought.

"I don't know," he said finally. "Got any tricks up your sleeve?"

She reacted instantly to his tone. "Don't snap at me," she warned. "It's not my fault that Velasquez got away again."

Garrett had been tottering on the edge so much lately that he felt as if he were going to slide off any second. He was spoiling for a fight. But picking one with her over this wouldn't be fair. He knew that.

"No—" he blew out a breath "—it's not."

In control again, he took out his cell phone and pressed one key. In less than ten seconds, he had Oscar on the line.

"Our fish swam upriver again." Out of the corner of his eye, he saw Megan looking around the huge room. Covering the bottom of the phone, he cautioned, "Don't touch anything."

It irritated Megan that he thought she needed the warning, and that he kept treating her like some bumbling novice when she'd been able to keep up with him every step of the way so far.

Maybe if she had been a little quicker instead of just keeping up, she would have Kathy by now, she thought. Frustrated, she made a face at him and went into the next room.

Like all the other rooms, in this house and in the one in Scottsdale, it was decorated completely in white. There wasn't a dash of color anywhere to break up the monotony. It was more of a mausoleum than a house.

Clearly the man had some sort of complex, she thought, needing to surround himself with so much unblemished-looking decor.

She heard Garrett entering behind her and turned around. He wasn't on the phone any longer.

"Anything?"

Guessing at Garrett's frustration, Oscar had mentioned a couple of potential leads, but nothing concrete yet. "Possibly."

"Are you going to tell me, or has our alliance been deep-sixed already?"

He would have liked to deep-six it, but had temporarily abandoned hope of doing so. "If I said yes, you'd only find a way to follow anyway."

She smiled at him then, and linked her arms through his. "Smart man, you're learning."

The display of friendship caught him off guard, but he managed to cover it.

He was also learning a few things about himself, things he wasn't about to share with her. Things he didn't want to even acknowledge to himself. But they were there nonetheless.

The unnerving fact that even at the height of all this, she kept worming her way into his mind, interfering with his focus, with his purpose. He didn't like that, didn't want it. Yet he kept returning to it with an unshakable curiosity.

He nodded toward the front door. It was time for them to leave. "The cleanup crew's on their way. If there's anything to learn, we'll know in a few hours."

That sounded logical enough. "What'll we do to entertain ourselves until then?"

A couple of things suggested themselves to him, fueled by the invitation in her voice. "You know, I can't quite figure you out."

Her eyes smiled at him before she did. "That's the general idea."

He shook his head, laughing shortly. "Always keep 'em guessing, is that it?"

Megan inclined her head, letting Garrett know that he'd guessed right, then added, "And never let them see you sweat."

But he wanted to, he thought. He really, really wanted to. He wanted to see and feel the damp sheen of perspiration along her body after a night of intense lovemaking.

"You up for something to eat?" he finally asked when his breath returned to his lungs.

He wanted her to be up for a lot of things, he realized. And therein lay the problem.

Looking at him, Megan sensed that he had the power to slash her concentration while heightening her awareness of things that had nothing whatsoever to do with recovering a runaway girl.

She wanted to let him know that he had that power, but knew she couldn't afford to.

If she did, it might very well be her downfall.

It was better this way, at least for her.

"Yes," she murmured, the look in her eyes giving away far more than she intended. "I'm up for something to eat."

Chapter 10

Megan found a telephone directory in the closet in the foyer. Flipping through the pages, she chose a restaurant based on the fact that it was close and that the food promised to be simple and good.

The choice surprised Garrett. He read the name above the pink-tipped nail as she pointed it out to him. It was the name of a popular chain throughout the Southwest.

He looked at her incredulously. "You like steak houses?"

She shrugged, replacing the directory. Except for the telephone book, the closet was empty. Like all the other closets in the house.

She closed the door. "I like steak. I figured you did, too."

Opening the front door for her, Garrett waited for

Megan to pass before going out himself. Steak was always his first choice, but she'd have no way of knowing that. It wasn't the kind of thing that was in his file.

"What makes you say that?"

She walked down the long driveway, holding her jacket closed against the sudden breeze coming from the desert. She should have brought something warmer with her, but who knew she was going to go traipsing around the countryside?

Megan looked at him. She figured that she had Wichita pretty well pegged, at least when it came to food. The rest, she was still working on.

"You're a complicated man, but your tastes are probably very basic and simple. No fine wines, no dishes that take six hours to prepare and have names you can't wrap your mouth around."

The only thing he knew that he was interested in wrapping his mouth around right now was walking next to him—and it bothered the life out of him.

Trying to block the feeling, Garrett crossed to the car first. "Am I being insulted?" He opened the door for her.

It would help a lot, he thought, if they could get back to arguing. But even that road seemed to have only one inevitable end.

"You're being observed," she corrected simply as she got into the car. Alerted by the sudden, rhythmic ringing coming from his pocket, she looked at his jacket. "You're also being paged."

He already had the cell phone in his hand. "Wichita.'' Garrett listened carefully, then nodded, remaining silent and giving nothing away.

Megan tried to interpret his expression, and got nowhere. It annoyed her not to be able to read him. She'd never cared for uncharted waters; she liked knowing exactly which direction the current was heading.

Garrett flipped the cell phone closed.

She looked at him impatiently as he walked around the front of the car and got in on the driver's side. ''Well?''

''The steak house is going to have to be put on hold.'' He had no time to sit and linger over a meal with her. And maybe that was all for the good. Garrett had a feeling that she was more than capable of dulling his edge. ''I've got to go.''

Did he expect her to get out of the car? And do what? Wait for a taxi?

''*We've* got to go,'' she corrected. He looked at her sharply. She was beginning to be able to read some of his expressions. This one was sheer annoyance. ''Temporary alliance, remember?''

Garrett blew out an exasperated breath. He began to say something, but he thought the better of it. ''I don't have time to sit here and argue with you.''

''Good, now you're being sensible.''

''I won't tell you what *you're* being,'' he muttered as he started the car.

''I'm being an asset,'' Megan pointed out cheerfully.

He laughed shortly. ''The first three letters enter

into the description, all right,'' he muttered under his breath.

She heard him, but since she'd gotten her way, Megan saw no reason to get into a heated discussion over his comment. Instead, she clipped on her seatbelt and sat back.

''Where are we off to?''

That ''we'' just didn't sound right, Garrett thought. Even temporarily.

''Reno.''

He tried to remember just where to catch the expressway from here. ''That was my real partner on the phone. The department just found out that the drop site has been changed to Reno.''

If he meant to put her in her place with the crack about his *real* partner, he could have saved his breath. It would take a great deal more than that. But something else he'd said did catch her attention.

''Drop?'' It was the first she'd heard of this added twist.

Garrett debated the wisdom of telling her, then decided that she'd find out on her own eventually if she tagged along long enough. ''Velasquez's supplier is coming in.''

Coming in. From out of town or out of the country? Obviously, since they were playing musical states, it had to be some distance away. Megan wondered if putting in a call to her ex-partner at the Bureau would yield anything. She and Murray had remained friendly, despite her abrupt career change.

She studied Garrett's profile. "You know who the supplier is?"

"We have our suspicions."

He knows, she thought. But if he wanted to keep that a secret, fine, she'd grant him that. It made no difference to her who the man or the organization was. All she wanted was Kathy.

There was no reason why his being close-mouthed should bother her.

But it did. A great deal.

Covering, Megan shrugged indifferently. "As long as I get to Kathy before anything goes down."

He knew from experience that things became hairy when nets finally closed. "You might not be able to."

Megan bristled. He was losing sight of things, so intent on the forest that he was oblivious to the trees that might be cut down. "She's fourteen years old—"

Garrett cut her off tersely. "So are a lot of other kids who are ODing on the white powder that slime is supplying."

Megan backed away. She'd learned a long time ago that she couldn't go through walls. But there had to be a door around somewhere. The trick was finding it.

"No argument." Taking a breath, she pointed to a hamburger drive-through coming up on the next block. "I'll spring for something to eat."

Garrett's first impulse was to just keep driving, but they were going to need to eat something. The trip ahead promised to be a long one.

"Put your money away," he told her, turning at the corner. "I'm buying."

"Yes, sir."

He ignored the grin he heard in her voice.

They'd been on the road for the last four hours, stopping only twice to refill the tank. He'd turned Megan down each time she'd offered to spell him and drive. Obviously the man was very possessive of his wheel.

She let him have his way. It was easier than arguing.

Megan blinked, prying her eyes open. The monotony of the road was threatening to lull her to sleep. The music coming from the radio wasn't helping. He had it set to a classical station. It was obvious that he preferred listening to talking. One endless piece linked into another, enhancing the drowsy atmosphere within the car. She felt her mind going numb.

His choice surprised her. If asked, she wouldn't have guessed that he was the type to like classical music. As for herself, she hated it—with a passion.

It finally got to be too much for her. Reaching over, she punched in another preset button, searching for something more appealing.

"What are you doing?" Garrett demanded. Moving her hand aside, he reset the radio.

"What does it look like I'm doing?" she snapped at him, her irritation getting the better of her. "I'm changing the station."

He knew damn well what she was doing, and he didn't like it. She seemed to enjoy interfering with every part of his life. "Leave it alone," he warned. "I like classical music."

"Well, I hate it." But she didn't try to change the station again. "It's putting me to sleep."

He didn't see how that was a bad thing. Awake, she might start talking again. "How can you hate classical music?"

Annoyed and restless, she stared out the window at the passing tumbleweeds. In the distance, there were the shadowy figures of broken and decaying cacti. "I just do, that's all."

With Mozart playing in the background, and nothing but the open road in front, Garrett glanced at her for a long moment. She'd said that with far too much passion for it to be an arbitrary matter of taste.

He made an educated guess. "Your father like classical music?"

Her shoulders stiffened. "Are we going back to Pysch 101 again?" she asked flippantly. And then, because Megan could feel his eyes on her as he waited for a response, she gave him one. "Yes, he did. He used to listen to it all the time."

It wasn't difficult for Garrett to piece things together. She'd been Daddy's little girl, and he had betrayed her trust. On top of that, when her father had stolen one of his children to keep with him, it hadn't been her. She'd been hurt on all fronts. He knew what that kind of hurt felt like.

"So," he said quietly, "you've sworn off everything that reminds you of your father."

Megan hated being analyzed, and lashed out before she could impose her own restraints. "Just because we're confined to a small space doesn't give you the right to probe and dissect me.''

''Hey, you're the one who invited yourself along, not me.''

The big jerk made it sound as if she'd done it on a whim. ''I'm not going along on a joyride. I'm trying to heal the rift in a family.''

''Will it help to heal your own?''

She had no intention of rebuilding anything that had once been. As far as she was concerned, you had to move on. And forward. ''It's too late for that.''

Twilight would be coming soon. Garrett figured they would reach the next town about an hour later. ''Seems to me that as long as you're breathing, it's not too late to make your peace with things.''

''I wouldn't preach if I were you.''

How had the ball suddenly been stolen from his court? ''And what's that supposed to mean?''

''You're going after Velasquez like it's your own personal crusade.''

Denial was on his lips, but he didn't say the words. ''Maybe it is.''

Megan had been blessed with more than a touch of curiosity, but it was usually directed toward things that could help her with cases. This time, it was more than that. Why had he pretended not to know what she meant? She wanted to put to rest her questions about this man.

''Why?''

''Maybe I don't like seeing young kids die.'' That should be enough for her, Garrett thought.

It wasn't. "But it's more than that, isn't it?"

For the first time in over a year, Garrett began to wish he hadn't given up smoking. She was really getting on his nerves. "Okay, you made your point. I don't probe you, you don't probe me."

"Uh-uh, you started this—"

"And now I'm finishing it, understand?" Garrett said tersely.

Megan understood all right. Understood that what was good for her wasn't reciprocated. Well, at least they were equal. That meant if she had to answer him, he had to return the favor.

But before she could drive her point home, she felt something. Megan stared at the car uncertainly. "What's that?"

Distracted, Garrett saw and heard nothing but the infuriating woman beside him.

"What's what?" she repeated.

The next moment, he felt it, too.

"That," she declared, pointing accusingly at the car's hood. "Why's the car shaking like that?" The car had suddenly begun vibrating. And it wasn't going anywhere. "What's wrong with it?"

Chewing on his anger, Garrett didn't answer her. He felt around under the dashboard.

"What are you looking for?"

"A way to make you stop asking questions," he snapped. "But that probably doesn't exist."

Finding the hood release, Garrett popped it, then got out and strode to the front of the car.

Perfect, just perfect, he thought darkly. Not only did

he have to put up with Megan and her ever-moving mouth, but now the car was giving him trouble as well. He should have traded the car in at the rental agency and gotten a newer one before he started on this leg of the trip. Hindsight was great.

Yanking up the hood, he looked down at an engine and components that looked even filthier in the creeping twilight. Garrett remembered seeing a flashlight in the glove compartment.

He turned to get it, and bumped right into Megan. Even through his anger, the contact made a quick, electric impression. He glared at her. "It's a large desert, why do you have to stand on top of me?"

"Don't yell at me because the car died."

"The car didn't die."

"It stopped moving, didn't it?" she accused.

"I'm not driving it, am I?"

The conversation was deteriorating. Megan was big enough to retreat first and focus on what was important. "Then you can fix it?" She ran her hands up and down her arms. It was beginning to get cooler.

Without answering, Garrett pulled a handkerchief from his back pocket and gingerly tapped a few engine parts.

"Well?" she asked.

Pointing the flashlight at the engine block, he saw the problem.

"It's the distributor cap." One corner of the plastic cap had been burned away, inhibiting contact with the spark plugs.

Megan had absolutely no idea what that meant. "Do we have a spare?"

He looked at her. "It's a distributor cap, not a tire."

"Sorry," she said icily, struggling to control her temper—because at least one of them should. "I don't know that much about cars."

"Obviously." Looking disgusted, he shut off the flashlight and shoved the handkerchief back into his pocket.

Megan bit her lower lip to keep from snapping back at him. Turning, she looked in the direction from which they'd just come. "We passed a truck stop about two miles back." She remembered seeing a gas station beside the diner as well as a couple of other buildings. "Maybe they have a spare distributor thing."

"Cap."

"A spare distributor cap," she enunciated. "Happy?"

Garrett was a long way from happy. But she was right. He shouldn't be taking it out in her.

"Sorry." Leaning in on the driver's side, Garrett took the keys out of the ignition. "Okay, let's go see about this truck stop. It's probably quicker to walk there than to call the rental agency's emergency repair hotline since we're probably not near any big garage." He stopped as he heard something. "Is that your stomach?"

Megan flushed. "I'm hungry."

"See if you can keep it down," he advised. "You might just attract the coyotes."

She looked around uneasily. She'd forgotten about the night life around here. "I didn't need that."

"Don't worry," he said. "I won't let them get you—unless they decide to go after me. Then you're on your own."

"My hero."

He laughed, taking the flashlight with him to help them find their way. "I try."

Megan frowned as she looked down at her plate. She knew that in reality she had a lot to be thankful for. They'd been lucky enough to have broken down close to a garage. The mechanic, who had to be summoned from the same diner they were now in, had gone back with them. And after looking over the problem, he promised to have them on the road again sometime tomorrow morning.

It worked out well in the time frame that Garrett was following, but that meant they had to spend the night in a place that wasn't even a speck on the map.

The anonymity and inconvenience wasn't what was bothering her. In all the excitement, she'd forgotten what today was. Until now.

Garrett watched her pick at her food from the moment the waitress set it down in front of Megan. He'd consumed his own meal quickly enough. The long trip, topped off by the walk, had driven his appetite to a new high.

The same, obviously, couldn't be said of hers, even though her stomach had been growling earlier.

"Food not to your liking?" Garrett finally asked as he finished his cup of coffee.

She looked at him then with the saddest eyes he'd ever seen. Instead of answering his question, she asked one of her own. "You know what today is?"

"Yeah." Garrett shrugged. The holiday bore no significance to him. One day was pretty much like another as far as he was concerned. "Thanksgiving. That's why the special's turkey." He nodded at the stained black menu board that hung on the rear wall.

He said it as if it was nothing. "And it doesn't bother you?"

He wiped his mouth with a corner of the napkin. "Why should Thanksgiving bother me?"

He was deliberately being obtuse, Megan thought. "Not Thanksgiving. Spending it on the road, in a diner that's two steps away from being condemned if there was such a thing as a board of health around here."

"Gotta spend it somewhere."

"Yes, but with your family." She sighed, looking around. Wichita just didn't understand. "See that man over there?" She nodded toward the solitary-looking man on the stool, bent over his meal.

Garrett looked over to size the stranger up, then turned back to Megan. "What about him?"

Didn't he see the loneliness, the desolation? "When I was a kid growing up, I always felt sorry for people like that. People who had no one to be with around the holidays. Who sat on solitary stools in dingy diners with no one to talk to, and ate dry turkey that stuck to the roof of their mouth." Fighting back a burst of emotion, she pushed her plate away from her. "And now I'm one of those people."

Garrett took a sip of water and then set the amber glass on the table.

"You're not sitting on a stool," he pointed out quietly. Her eyes shifted to his, and he felt a tightness in his throat. He slipped his hand over hers. "And you're not alone."

Something very warm slid through Megan. Warm and demanding. "You?"

"Me. I'm with you." There was something in her sadness that spoke to Garrett. That made him want to chase it away. "Last I checked, I qualified as a human being."

Megan smiled at him, grateful for what he was trying to say.

"Yeah, maybe you do at that." She rallied, pulling herself together. This was out of character for her. She didn't usually let her emotions get the better of her, especially not around others. "Sorry, I didn't mean to grow all soft and sloppy on you."

"That's all right." He went back to eating his meal. "It's nice to see you have a human side yourself."

"Maybe," she allowed as she looked at him, "at times I'm a little too human for my own good."

And mine, he thought.

He nodded toward her plate. "The gravy isn't half bad. Try putting it on the turkey."

He was making an effort, Megan thought. The least she could do was meet him halfway. She smiled. "Maybe I will."

Chapter 11

"More coffee?"

The tired-looking waitress directed the question toward them from behind the counter. She held up a glass pot half filled with light brown liquid that Megan could see through even from where she sat.

They were the last two people in the diner, besides the waitress. The short-order cook had left twenty minutes ago.

Megan shook her head in reply. The cup she'd been nursing had long since grown cold. It hadn't been much of a help in sliding the last piece of apple pie down. The pie had tasted stale. She'd split it with Garrett, but he hadn't seemed to notice, consuming his half with gusto. She wondered if he was accustomed to food like that. Given his life on the road, it was probably a good guess.

She had no idea why she had a sudden urge to make him a real home-cooked meal.

"I've already had enough coffee to keep me up all night. Which," she glanced at Garrett, "I guess is a good thing, seeing as how we have no place to stay."

Crepe shoes squeaked across the cracked vinyl floor as the waitress approached their table. Megan noticed that the woman's coat was draped over the last stool at the counter. Mechanically, the woman, whose name tag proclaimed her to be Maude, picked up the last of their plates.

There was a hint of guilt in Maude's voice as she said, "Well, I'm afraid I've got to lock up now. It's Thanksgiving." She nodded toward the single decoration on the counter as if that verified her statement. "And I promised my Henry to be home before seven."

"Her Henry" had turned out to be the mechanic who'd towed Garrett's vehicle back to his cluttered, single-bay garage.

Garrett looked at Megan. The truck stop had nothing in the way of overnight accommodation. "I guess we should go back to the car. We could try sleeping in it," he suggested. It looked like their only option, since they weren't going anywhere at the moment.

Maude looked appalled at the thought. "It's too cold for that. Temperature's dropping all the time," she said, picking up their plates.

Even if it wasn't, there was another problem with the solution. "It's in Henry's garage, remember?"

Megan reminded him. ''Which means we can't get at it anyway.''

Maude chewed on a wide lower lip that had seen over half a century of bright red lipstick. ''Hold on a minute.'' Shuffling to the counter, she deposited their dishes and kept on walking. ''I'll be right back.'' Maude disappeared through the single swinging door into the kitchen.

Megan frowned into her coffee cup. In a few hours, she'd probably be longing for this, but right now she couldn't force herself to finish it. She set the cup down and looked at Garrett.

''What do you suppose she's up to?''

Garrett could predict the actions of men far better than he could those of any woman. He shrugged. ''Maybe she's trying to find a place for us in the freezer.''

For a split second, Megan was seven again, sitting beside her older brother and watching shadowy creatures on the television screen. An icy feeling slid up and down her spine. It took a minute to remind herself that she didn't believe in things that went *bump* in the night. But she'd learned that there were people out there who were a lot scarier than any parade of Saturday-afternoon monsters had ever been.

''That's not as funny as it sounds,'' she told him. He arched a quizzical brow. ''You obviously weren't raised on horror movies.''

Megan kept an eye on the swinging door, waiting for Maude's return. She thought she heard the woman talking to someone—except that the cook had already gone home. "That's how they got the original Blob, you know. Freezing it to death."

"No," he said, studying her. "I didn't know. Just how much trivia do you carry around inside that head of yours?"

She grinned. Like an ever-growing sponge, Megan had a mind that absorbed everything she came in contact with. And remembered it. "You'd be surprised."

"No," the answer was honest and emphatic. "I wouldn't be."

Garrett was beginning to think that nothing about Megan Andreini would really surprise him anymore. The woman was an ongoing surprise, which contradictorily, he reasoned, made surprise predictable.

She was an enigma.

"I just called Henry," Maude announced, returning. Her guilty expression had faded. "He said you can stay in the back room at the garage if you promise not to mess with anything." She pressed her lips together, embarrassed over the warning she'd been told to deliver. "I know you won't." Struggling into the coat she'd brought over with her, she continued. "It's got a cot." Maude looked over her shoulder in surprise, as Garrett helped her find her other sleeve and then slid the coat into place. She smiled warmly at him. "Sometimes we stay there during the rainy season when the storm gets too nasty and we can't get home."

Picking up her purse, she led the way to the front door, then waited until they both walked out. "I'd invite you there—to the house—but Henry's family came, and we're full up as it is.'' She locked the diner. "Lord knows it's small even just for the two of us.''

"There's no need to apologize,'' Garrett assured the woman. "You've done more than enough as it is. The room'll be fine.''

It would have to be, he thought.

But he had to admit that he had some doubts about it when Maude unlocked the garage and led them to the tiny back room. It hardly seemed like a room at all; it was more of an oversize closet doubling as a storage unit. There were pungent, grease-stained coveralls in a pile in the corner of the floor, and the cot itself was buried beneath stacks of old newspapers. Scattered, empty metal cans on the floor made moving around difficult.

Maude flushed as she surveyed the garage. "I know it doesn't look like there's enough room there for a couple.'' She gestured toward the cot. "But Henry and I used to make do.''

By the reminiscent smile on Maude's lips, Megan gathered that Henry was a great deal more spry than he appeared at first glance.

"And we will, too,'' Garrett told Maude. Gently, he ushered the woman to the front of the garage. "Now you'd better get home to Henry and his family. We've kept you long enough.''

Maude smiled at him. She leaned her face up to his and whispered, "Tell your wife she's got herself a charmer.'' Patting his arm, she added in a louder voice, "Henry'll be here in the morning to work on that car of yours.'' Confidence shone in her eyes. "Have you on your way in no time.''

Garrett certainly hoped so. The alternative, he thought as he helped Maude pull down the corrugated garage door and fix it in place, was to put in a call and have someone come and get them in the morning. He preferred not to appear as if he needed bailing out.

Garrett turned around to assess his surroundings. He'd been in gloomier-looking places—although not recently. There was a single light fixture hanging from the center of several crossed beams. The corrugated roof, a good fifteen feet above them, must have made heating and cooling the place an impossible dream.

The naked bulb cast eerie shadows everywhere. Their car, the only other occupant, was standing in the middle of the garage. It appeared that business was slow for Henry. Given that the man looked to be in his seventies, Garrett figured Henry probably liked it that way.

He picked his way back to Megan, taking care not to trip over the wrenches and tools that were flung haphazardly about.

"It's not exactly the way I pictured spending the night,'' Garrett said, directing his voice toward the back room.

"Oh?''

He heard something crash and hurried the rest of the way to the back.

Megan walked out of the back room carrying an armload of newspapers. She'd taken off her jacket and pushed up her sleeves, obviously digging in. Passing him, she crossed to the workbench and deposited the newspapers against the wall behind it.

She pushed her hair out of her eyes with the back of her hand. "And just how did you picture spending the evening?"

Puzzled, he followed Megan back into the room, entering just in time to see her bend over to pick up another stack of papers. Her cherry-red skirt moved with her, sliding up the remainder of her leg and giving him an eyeful.

No doubt about it, he thought, the woman had an incredible build.

Watching her, Garrett realized exactly how he'd pictured the evening—maybe not this one, but some evening.

Soon.

He laughed shortly to himself, shaking his head. If he wasn't careful, he was going to lose his grip. "You don't want to know."

Megan turned around, newspapers stacked in her arms. There was a look in his eyes that she didn't want to analyze. It gave her butterflies.

"Maybe you're right."

He followed her out again as she repeated the routine. "What are you doing?"

Putting the pile down, she went in for the third and last one, then set it up beside the first two. She dusted off her hands. "Cleaning."

Garrett could see that. "Why?"

Finished with the newspapers, Megan tackled the dirty coveralls. They smelled of sweat, gasoline and

several things she couldn't place; she figured she was
better off that way.

"Because when I'm edgy, I clean. When I'm wired,
I clean. And, when I'm restless—" arms loaded with
coveralls that she really didn't want to be this close
to, she pushed past him "—I clean. Right now, I'm
edgy, wired and restless."

She dropped one pair of coveralls. Garrett stooped
and picked it up the way he might a piece of evidence:
very gingerly and by the edge. "Maybe he should pay
us instead of the other way around tomorrow."

She stopped putting the dirty coveralls into what she
assessed to be the designated hamper.

"'Us'?" she echoed. "Are you planning on cleaning up with me?"

Garrett tossed the coveralls on top of the others.
That about did it for him, he thought. She wanted to
play at being the cleaning woman, the job was all hers.

"Figure of speech." He took out his handkerchief
and wiped his hand. "You wanted me to think of this
as a partnership, didn't you?" He indicated the garage.
"This is where your end of it can take over."

Megan gave him a disapproving look. "You mean
you could sleep in a place like this?" But then, he was
a typical male, she thought. Most men were oblivious
to dirt and filth.

Garrett shrugged. "I can't sleep anyplace but in my
own bed. So it wouldn't matter to me how clean you
got that room in the back, I'm still not going to be
able to get much sleep."

She wouldn't have thought that he had trouble

sleeping anywhere. He seemed a man who could make do under any conditions, and it was hard picturing him with insomnia.

Megan picked up the socket wrench closest to her on the floor. ''I guess that settles the problems of who gets the cot.''

Garrett saw a radio over by the windowsill. Crossing to it, he switched it on. ''There was never any problem over that. You were getting it.''

''Chivalry?'' Megan braced herself for another on-slaught of classical music. Instead, he left it on a station that played a mixture of old and new. The small, thoughtful act touched her. ''Your mother taught you well. I'm sure she'd be proud of you.''

He shoved his hands into his pockets, looking out the window. Or trying to. The thick layer of dirt and grime, combined with darkness, made it impossible to see anything. Garrett dismissed her words. ''That's not possible.''

''Why?'' Opening the top drawer in the tool chest, Megan found it empty—which wasn't a surprise. She placed the smaller wrenches into it. ''You're not that much of a blackguard.''

Garrett turned around to look at her. There was a smudge on her nose. Without thinking, he crossed to her and, holding her chin in one hand, used his thumb to wipe away the smudge. ''Where the hell do you get these words from? 'Heretofore.' 'Blackguard.'''

When he touched her, he made things happen in-side. Things like tiny explosions of electricity and lights. Megan drew her head away. Slowly.

"I read, Wichita. Books without pictures. I realize that might be a new concept for you." She put some distance between them so that she could resume breathing normally again. Somehow the air seemed to evaporate every time they were that close. "And why can't your mother be proud of you?"

"She's not around anymore."

His voice was flat. Emotionless. She heard the emotions anyway, and realized she'd misstepped. "Oh. I'm sorry. I didn't mean to dig up anything painful."

Garrett didn't want her pity. Pity made him feel small, weak, vulnerable. And he'd taken great pains not to be. Ever.

"It's not painful, it's just in the past."

No, it isn't, she thought. "How about your father?"

Garrett shrugged. "Same place."

There was something about the way he said it that caught her attention. "Did they die together?"

She wasn't going to stop until she got the whole thing, was she? Garrett thought. "Flash flood when I was thirteen. Satisfied?"

She turned her back on him as she bent down to pick up another tool. "You know, if the DEA ever gives classes on attitude adjustment, I suggest you at least sit in on a session or two." She threw the tool into the second drawer. "Maybe the whole semester."

He didn't need to be lectured by her about attitude. She wasn't exactly getting an award for Miss Congeniality. "Yeah, maybe I will." He watched as she deposited another handful of tools into the next drawer. "Now what are you doing?"

The lighting here wasn't *that* bad. Why did he have to keep asking? "Putting his tools away."

He shut the drawer before she could fit in any more. "Did it ever occur to you that Henry might not want to have them put away? That he wants them where they are?" He could tell by her expression that the thought never even crossed her mind. "He said not to 'mess' with anything, remember? You don't mess with a man's tools, Megan."

"I'm not 'messing' with them." She yanked open the drawer and put more tools in. "I'm getting them off the floor so one of us doesn't trip over them during our stay here at the Desert Excelsior." Exasperated, she slammed the drawer shut again. "What *is* the name of this place, anyway?"

"I don't think it has one. A garage, a diner and a souvenir stand that hasn't seen a paying customer in probably a decade doesn't qualify for a name."

Megan willed the tension from her shoulders. There was no reason, she told herself, to feel this tense. No reason at all. She'd been in worse places, dirtier places, and certainly smaller ones than this drafty barn-like enclosure.

It wasn't the place, it was the company.

Worse, it was her.

She turned away from him and looked at the window behind the radio. "How long do you suppose it's been since that window was washed?"

"I don't even think it's a window. Looks more like greasy butcher paper." He caught her hands as she started to walk over to the tiny closet that served as a bathroom. "You don't have to wash it. You don't have to clean anything," he told her.

He said it, she thought, as if he knew what was going on in her head.

Garrett looked down at the hands he was holding. "You're getting dirty."

She shrugged, wishing he would let go. "You touch grease, you get dirty."

Her eyes looked dark green in this light, he thought. Dark green and beautiful. "Very profound."

He was teasing her again. Megan pulled free. "I'm not at my best right now."

"Matter of opinion."

His eyes were touching her, even if his hands weren't. She had to remind herself to breathe.

"Yours being?"

His smile was slow, and it wove its way under her skin with terrifying accuracy.

"I think you rise to the occasion no matter what, Megan Andreini. You don't strike me as a woman who stands there as life rolls over her. *You* do the rolling, not life."

Her mouth felt dry. Maybe she should have gotten a drink-to-go. "Okay, I have to warn you that while I do like it, sweet talk has never been known to make me change my mind about anything."

"What makes you think I'm trying to get you to change your mind about anything?"

She wanted an argument, something to hang on to. Something to block the thoughts she was having. "Oh, like you don't want me to turn around and go back to Bedford.''

"Not particularly. At least,'' he amended, "not tonight.'' He cut the distance that she had put between them. "You'd have to walk, and I'd have to be pretty damn heartless to let you.''

She wanted to back away. But backing away was cowardly, and she'd never been a coward. So she stood her ground. Until the ground they shared was one.

Her pulse racing, she looked up into his eyes and saw herself reflected there. The man could have been a magician.

She ran her tongue along her lips. It didn't help. "And you're not pretty damn heartless?''

Taking her hand in his, he pressed it against his chest. "You tell me.''

The room got a little darker. And a little warmer. She tried to be flippant and only half succeeded. "Nope, there's a heart there all right. And it's beating. Rather hard.'' It was difficult, forming the words. Difficult when all she wanted to do was kiss him and lose herself in him. "Why is that, Wichita?''

The press of her fingers against his chest quickened his pulse. And his desire. Ever so slowly, he rubbed his cheek against hers, breathing in the faint scent of perfume and shampoo.

"You tell me,'' he whispered again into her hair.

A shiver frantically worked its way along her spine. And a deep need worked its way to the surface. A need to be held, to forget that this was just a solitary night in the middle of nowhere, and that in the morning they would go their separate ways—emotionally if not physically.

A need to believe that wonderful things did still happen and that these kinds of feelings could last forever.

She could feel her eyes fluttering shut as his breath skimmed along her neck. "Sometimes," she said with effort, "I don't want to talk."

She felt his smile along her throat as he pressed a kiss there. "That's like saying you don't want to breathe." He raised his head and looked at her, his eyes meeting hers. "I want you, Megan."

The simplicity, the honesty in the words, made her feel like crying. She didn't know why. "I wouldn't have guessed."

He kissed her lips, a soft, tender kiss that spoke of temporary truce as well as desire. "I believe in being subtle."

Megan wound her arms around his neck. "Like a train wreck." Standing on her toes, she pressed her mouth urgently against his.

It was, Garrett realized distantly, like the opening of the gate at Pamplona and having the bulls suddenly charge, taking the street. Desire broke free, taking him prisoner in its stead and holding him fast.

He could feel the outline of her body as it burned against his. Needs and emotions twisted within him, each striving to win out. Each wanting possession of him, even as they urged him to take possession of her.

He kissed her eyes, her throat, her cheeks, her lips

as his hands moved along her body, touching her, wanting her. He couldn't find a place to settle; each new place enticed him to move on, to take more, and then to retrace and reclaim.

With each caress along her body, through her hair, along her face, Megan found herself burning for him even more than she had a moment before. It was like having him stoke a fire inside her. She had no idea that there was this crying need within her, this over-whelming desire to be made love to. To make love to and with a man.

To and with…Garrett.

With an eagerness that seldom marked any part of her private life, Megan undid his belt and yanked fran-tically at his shirt until she'd pulled it free. She didn't even remember working the buttons out of their holes. All she knew was that she wanted to feel him against her, to have his cool skin soothe her feverish one.

And all the while, his mouth was working tiny mir-acles over hers: giving, taking, teasing.

Just as his kiss deepened, making her head spin, he retraced his path and brought his lips to her throat, to her neck, to the swell of her breasts. There wasn't a single part of her that wasn't on fire. That didn't want him.

As she pulled his shirt from his shoulders, she felt Garrett's hands on either side of her thighs, moving underneath her skirt. She drew her breath in sharply as she felt his fingers skimming along the outline of her underwear. Over and over again, making her crazy, until she finally felt him touch her intimately.

The climax that soared through her took her completely by surprise.

Garrett looked at her as her eyes opened wide with wonder, her body stiffening, then shuddering against him. Fists of desire slammed into him, pushing him on.

Each shred of excitement she exhibited only made him that much more aroused himself, that much more dedicated to making this the most memorable encounter she'd ever experienced.

He wanted her to remember him. Always. The way he would always remember her.

"Do dingy garages always turn you on like this?" he asked teasingly against her ear.

Megan shivered as she felt his tongue outline her ear, driving a salvo of pleasure through her. She gripped his shoulders.

"Just the smell of gasoline," she quipped back.

The next moment, their lips sealed to one another again, she felt herself being picked up in his arms. The weightless feeling only enhanced the wildness throbbing throughout her body. Her heart was slamming so hard against her rib cage that she half believed it was going to create a hole and fall out.

She didn't care. All she cared about was this feeling rushing through her. And this man making love with her.

He set her down on the cot, joining her in the limited space. There was just enough room for their bodies to tangle together. To fuse.

Garrett undressed her, his fingers flying under a

power all their own. Nude, her skin looked like heated vanilla ice cream against the dark blanket. He'd always had a weakness for ice cream, and vanilla had been the first flavor he'd ever tasted.

He devoured her, making love to her with every fiber of his body. Making everything within her sing. Bringing her to peak after peak with the expert movement of his body against hers.

Garrett made love to her with his eyes, with his mouth, with his very breath. Over and over again, he possessed her body before he ever entered it.

Finally, her body racked with exquisite explosions that left her exhausted and wanting more, Megan looked up at him.

"If you're trying to get me to cry 'uncle,'" she told him breathlessly, just barely holding on, "you're going to have to try harder."

Garrett grinned. He couldn't hold back any longer. It wasn't humanly possible. "I always rise to the challenge."

The smile on her lips as she accepted him was something halfway between mischievous and ethereal. And it would brand him forever.

"Nice to know," she murmured against his mouth before there was no more time for words. And nothing left of her but pure, raw longing and desire.

They rode over the crests together, faster and faster, enjoying the ride, longing for journey's end and yet wanting to keep it at bay for a few more eternities.

And when it ended, and they were spent, the holding was almost as wondrous as any of what went before.

For just a little while, they had found a haven. Together.

Chapter 12

"His name was Andy."

Locked safely in the arms of contentment and on the verge of drifting asleep, Megan roused herself as Garrett's words cut through the silence. Opening her eyes, she turned toward him.

"Pardon?"

Garrett figured she'd done something to him with her lovemaking, touched something that had curled itself into a ball to avoid contact. He spoke before he could think better of it and stop himself. He spoke because he needed to.

"Back at the hospital that night, you asked me who I'd lost to Velasquez. His name was Andy. Andy Wichita." It had been a long time since he'd said the full name aloud. Fifteen years. Garrett looked at her. "He was my brother."

She laid a hand on his shoulder, her eyes eloquently saying what her lips could only attempt. "Oh, Wichita, I'm so sorry."

He'd schooled himself to shun sympathy if it came his way. And so it usually didn't.

Yet he couldn't bring himself to recoil from hers. He needed it. But the glimpse of weakness scared the hell out of him.

He talked because he didn't want to think. Because for a little while, talking about Andy almost made it seem as if he was still alive.

"He was my older brother. Not by much, just eleven months. But when we were kids that made him top dog." The faint smile of remembrance faded. "When we lost our parents, he couldn't handle it. Couldn't handle being alone with me to look after."

He'd told her that he was thirteen when his parents died. That would have made his brother fourteen. And both of them candidates for foster homes. "But you were both underage, weren't you?"

He shook his head. "Didn't matter. Andy felt responsible. And he needed a crutch to deal with it, or try to deal with it." Andy had always been too fun-loving, too scattered, to be responsible. "Velasquez was little more than a street dealer then, in Texas. Hadn't found his 'high class niche' yet." Garrett's lips curled contemptuously. "Andy started stealing to pay for his habit." It had started out with little things from the foster homes they stayed in, then gradually grew. Garrett had covered for him when he could, had taken the blame for his brother when he couldn't. "Hating himself for what he'd become. Hating me for getting him there...."

And Megan could see that the blame had eaten away at him. "But you didn't—"

Garrett ignored her protest, aching for the brother he'd lost. Swearing vengeance for the umpteenth time on the man who'd stolen his brother from him.

"Velasquez had made him one of his runners. One day Andy just couldn't take it anymore. Couldn't take what he'd become." The words felt like lead on his tongue, but Garrett pushed on. He needed to tell her about his brother. "He scraped together just enough money to buy the amount of cocaine he needed to end all his pain. And then he did." Garrett turned his face toward her then, his eyes hard, filled with his own agony. Agony that hadn't released its hold on him in all these years. "That's what I've got against Velasquez. And that's why I won't stop until he's permanently behind bars. Or dead."

She looked at him for a long moment. "Will you stop then?"

"What do you mean?" He had no idea what she was talking about. "Of course I'll stop."

Megan wasn't so sure. She propped herself up on her elbow, peering into his face. "Will you? Will you stop blaming yourself for Andy's death?"

"I don't blame myself," he said angrily.

She didn't hear his words. She heard something else, something far more basic in his denial. Something she'd endured herself.

Trying to reach him, she softened her expression.

''It wasn't your fault, you know. You can only help so much, be there so much. If the other person doesn't want to take it, there's nothing you can do.''

''I don't know what you're talking about,'' he said with disgust as he turned away from her.

''Yes, you do. I wanted to be there for my mother more than anything in the world, but she shut me out. Shut me out because I wasn't Chad. I wasn't the child who had been kidnapped from her.''

Garrett looked at her and saw that it cost her to tell him. She'd drawn him back, not with the touch of her hand, but with what she shared.

''The fact that there were still two of us at home, needing her, didn't counterbalance the one who wasn't. And there was nothing I could do to make it any better for her.''

Megan took his face between her hands, aching for him, for the lost boy he'd been, who perhaps still lived within the tough-as-nails man he'd become. Very slowly, she brought her lips to his and kissed him. Not with passion and unbridled desire, but with under-standing, empathy and another emotion that was far larger than both. One she wouldn't put a name to be-cause she'd once sworn never to care about anyone else without safeguards in place.

The sweetness Garrett received, that he tasted in her kiss, undid him more completely than the passion had. His arms closed around her, drawing Megan to him, bringing fire to the kiss and to the night. He lost him-self in her, truly lost himself and his pain.

For a little while.

* * *

The hint of sunlight, struggling to push its way into the room through the grimy window, gave Garrett his first clue that somehow it had gotten to be morning.

As he blinked to chase away the last remnants of sleep, it suddenly came to him that he *had* actually fallen asleep. Here, in a crammed cot that was probably meant to accommodate an adolescent boy at best, he'd fallen asleep. Fallen asleep with Megan's body cradled against his, as if they were two spoons in a drawer.

He'd slept somewhere else, through most of the night, in a bed that wasn't his. Garrett wasn't sure just exactly what that meant. Didn't know if he *wanted* to know.

All he did know was that he should have been up hours ago. Leaning over Megan, he shook her shoulder. "Megan, it's morning."

The voice in Megan's ear broke apart the wonderful dream she was having. A warm, silken dream that had curled itself around her, culminating in the feel of a man's arm wrapped around her. Holding her.

Keeping her safe.

"Hmm?" The lazy sigh abruptly vanished as she opened her eyes and then bolted upright. "Oh, my God, what time is it?"

Garrett looked at his watch, then raised his eyes to her. The answer evaporated on a tongue that had gone instantly dry at the sight of her. The blanket had dropped to her waist when she'd sat up. Seeing her, nude and as perfect as anything he'd ever laid eyes on, made him want to make love to her all over again.

Get a grip, Wichita. She's just a woman, not a habit.

The silent admonishment made him realize that he already wanted her to be a habit.

His habit.

He turned from her as he put on his clothes, shutting out the sight, if not the desire. Garrett knew if he looked at her, he wouldn't want to leave this room. Not for a long time.

"It's late," he snapped in reply. "Get your clothes on. We've got to get going."

His coldness stung. It was worse than any of his earlier displays. Worse, because Megan had thought that they actually shared more than their bodies last night.

Grabbing her clothes from the floor, Megan rallied. Fine. If all she'd been last night was a tumble in the hay, then two could play at this game. She slid on her underwear and skirt, killing angry tears.

She'd been a fool to think that she felt anything for him anyway.

"Is the car running yet?" She punched her arms through her sweater, wishing the open space was Garrett's face instead.

"I don't know."

Megan ran her fingers through her hair impatiently as she moved past him. The small space made maneuvering difficult—and reminded her of just how warm, hard and tempting his body had felt against hers last night.

Damn it, don't go there, she upbraided herself.

"Excuse me." Elbowing him out of her way, she opened the door to the rest of the garage.

Henry was already there, bent over the engine as the hood yawned open over his head. Megan took comfort in his presence.

"Good morning." Megan addressed the old man's back as she ventured forward. "How's the patient?"

Looking at her over his shoulder, Henry drew the white tufts that passed for eyebrows together in a single line.

"The car." Megan pointed to it. "How's it doing?"

"Oh." He chuckled to himself. "It'll live. Got the cap in." He gestured at something in the engine Megan wouldn't have been able to identify if her life depended on it. "Not the same brand, but it'll get you to where you're going if you don't push it." He ducked back down to continue working, his permanently stained fingers wrapped around a socket wrench. "By the way, the wife sent over coffee if you're interested." Extending his hand behind him, Henry waved the wrench in the general direction of the scarred wooden table.

Out of the corner of her eye, Megan saw Garrett entering. She deliberately avoided looking his way as she crossed to the coffeepot warming on the single burner. She poured the coffee into one of the paper cups Henry had brought along. Megan took a sip. The coffee tasted surprisingly good.

"That was very nice of her. How much do we owe you? For the cot and room service?" she said, smiling.

He didn't answer immediately as he worked to tighten a cable. "You the one who cleaned up my stuff?"

She wasn't sure whether the question was an accusation, or just part of the conversation. In either case, there was no point in denying it or pretending she didn't know what he was talking about. The man was too old to believe in elves. "Yes."

He nodded to himself more than to her. "Thought as much. Can't remember when it's been this clear on the floor. Pay me for the distributor cap and we'll call it even." Straightening, he blew his nose in the huge handkerchief he kept tucked in his back pocket, then stood back to admire the car. "It's running."

Megan breathed a sigh of relief. She couldn't wait to put this place, and its tiny back room, behind her.

They were on the road again within the hour, an uneasy silence riding along with them. It had crept inside the moment they were both sitting in the vehicle, and remained, growing larger, for more than half an hour.

It was finally broken, not by either one of them nor the radio that he'd left on, but by the ring of Garrett's cell phone.

Apparently it was in operating order again, Garrett thought, taking the phone out of his pocket and flipping it open. "Wichita."

"Where have you been?" he heard Oscar demand. "I've been trying to get through all night. We thought you were down."

The choice of words brought an involuntary smile to Garrett's lips. Maybe he had been—for a while. But he was up now. Up and focused. All that mattered, he insisted silently, was bringing in Velasquez.

"Not down, just out of range, Oscar. I had car trouble. The distributor cap had to be replaced," he added, although what Oscar knew about cars could be crammed into a thimble. His partner's expertise lay with computers, not engines.

"You okay now?"

Garrett slanted a look toward Megan. No, he was far from okay—but he would be. "The mechanic thought we could make it to the next town. I figure I'll rent another car when I get there. Why were you trying to reach me?"

Even as he asked, Garrett braced himself for another change in plans. Everything had been in a state of constant flux ever since he'd started on this assignment. Including him.

"Just to let you know that everything's on track and still on. Velasquez and his men just entered the city. We've got people all over, and one of them spotted the white limo pulling up to the hotel."

"Hotel?" This was a change in venue, Garrett thought, even though the news, for once, was good. Were there others?

"Yeah, seems like he's staying at a hotel until this goes down. Maybe he couldn't unload the other two properties and he's strapped for cash," Oscar joked. And then his voice sobered. "Or maybe this time, this is really it."

Garrett realized that Megan had shifted in her seat so that her back was to him. Before he could wonder why, he heard the melodious chimes of a telephone number being dialed on a cell phone keypad. Megan was placing a call to someone.

He tried to keep his mind on what Oscar was telling him. "Where's Velasquez staying?"

"The Excelsior. Tower suites, top floor," Oscar added. "I guess he thinks he's the king of the world...."

Who is she calling? Garrett wondered. With Oscar talking in his ear, he couldn't hear Megan's voice. And he'd just missed what Oscar had said. "What?"

"I said, maybe he'll get high on his own stuff and try to fly. It'd save us all a lot of time and money."

This time, he heard the weariness in Oscar's voice. A lot of man-hours had gone into this. The only difference was that the others involved had a life to get back to. This *was* his life, his purpose.

"Not him. He's too smart to take any of that garbage into his system." And if he were being truthful with himself, Garrett didn't want Velasquez put out of commission before he got to him. That honor *belonged* to him, and he wouldn't be cheated of it. "Anything else new?"

"No, the drop's still set for tomorrow night."

A little more than twenty-four hours, and then it would all be over. He glanced toward Megan, who was still on the phone.

All of it.

"Stay in touch if there's anything new," he told Oscar. "I should reach Reno in another four hours."

"Try not to break down again," Oscar warned dryly.

"Don't worry," Garrett said tersely. "I won't."

It was a promise to himself that he meant to keep.

Flipping the phone closed, he tucked it back into his pocket, then glanced at Megan. Her voice was low, but without Oscar talking in his ear, he could hear her.

"Right, Kathy'll be home soon, I promise. Yes, in Reno. Keep a light burning in the window, Mr. Teasdale. And one in your heart."

When she closed the phone and put it away, she could feel Garrett's eyes on her, but she refused to look at him or initiate any conversation. She could hold out just as long as he could.

Longer even.

"Isn't that a little too positive sounding?"

It figured that the first thing out of his mouth would be criticism. Megan worked at holding her temper—and her perspective. Served her right for being sympathetic to a man whose heart came packaged with a Teflon warranty.

She raised her chin. "Right now, nothing sounds too positive to those people."

She was thinking of the moment; he was thinking of the future. All he could focus on was the way the couple would feel if Megan failed. "What if you can't deliver? What if something goes wrong?" he pressed. "What then?"

Leave it to him to only see the dark side of it, Megan thought. Couldn't he put himself in someone else's shoes for a minute? Couldn't he spare a little compassion, or be optimistic, for that matter?

"I'll face it when it comes," she said fiercely, then got her temper under control. "And nothing's going to go wrong." She looked at him pointedly. "No matter what." She was putting him on notice that she was going to get Kathy out, no matter what happened to his plans for Velasquez's downfall.

"And for your information, I think those people need an extra dose of hope right around now. They've just faced Thanksgiving without their daughter, worried that this is the beginning of the rest of their lives, not a temporary separation. For better or for worse, I'm all they have to find Kathy." Despite her best intentions, her temper broke free of its bonds. "I'd rather give them something to hang on to than cover my own tail." She glared at him, daring Garrett to argue. "I suppose you think I'm stupid."

Garrett had been quiet during her outburst. Quiet and thoughtful. Listening to her, he was beginning to discover, got him further than arguing.

"I think a lot of things, Megan." His tone was as mild as hers was filled with emotion. Garrett looked at her for a second before continuing. "But one thing I don't think is that you're stupid."

She looked at him in confusion. Every time she had him pegged, he shifted the picture. She blew out a breath, still staring straight ahead. "Don't start being nice to me, Wichita. You'll just mix me up again."

Garrett smiled to himself. "Maybe that's the plan."

She looked at him then, the expression on her face telling him that she was willing to meet him halfway—if he remained civilized. He figured maybe compromise was good for the soul. "Music?" He switched on the radio.

Megan looked at it warily. She was in no mood to put up with memories of the distant past. "Classical?"

He pushed in a button. She recognized the song. "Modern."

It was a compromise. Maybe there was hope for the man, after all. Megan sat back in her seat, the stiffness leaving her shoulders. "Okay."

Garrett was a man who knew when to keep his mouth shut. Usually. But somehow, Megan seemed to blow apart all the rules. All he wanted her to do was understand—even if he couldn't.

"Look, about last night—"

Oh no, she'd just pushed that into the background, Megan thought. She wasn't about to go over it again. They'd just struck up a truce; she didn't want him saying anything that would send them both back to their corners. She felt too tired, too edgy, to handle anything that would come of a confrontation.

So she cut him off. "No explanations necessary, Wichita. We were cold. We did the logical thing to stave it off." She shrugged carelessly. "We kept warm enough to make it through to morning."

Garrett doubted that that was the way she really saw it. He certainly didn't. "I figure we kept warm enough to heat an entire Alaskan village through a blizzard."

A smile crept over her lips, but she kept her face

forward, her eyes on the road. "Never do anything halfway—that's my motto."

And last night hadn't been halfway. Not for either of them. "Got any other mottoes I should know about?"

The smile wouldn't leave. It was there when she spared him half a glance. "Maybe."

Suddenly, the future that loomed before him became a whole lot more promising. And a great deal more complicated than he liked. He was torn over which way to lean.

The car shuddered. Megan caught her breath, holding it to see what would happen next. But the shudder was isolated, and the vehicle kept going. Maybe their luck would hold.

Megan leaned forward a little, her hand on the dashboard. "Henry said that he thought this could get us to where we had to go."

"Operative word here is *thought.*"

"We have to hope," she replied.

It was all they had, she thought, and it wasn't really grounded in reality. But if they held onto it—if *she* held onto it—maybe everything would turn out all right.

It had been a long time since there'd been hope in her own life.

Chapter 13

Megan let out a long breath. They had gotten into the city on a tire and a prayer, but at least they'd made it.

Ten miles outside Reno, the car had begun to shimmy and shake like a building at the epicenter of an earthquake. It was touch-and-go as to whether they'd get to the city. The car finally gave up the ghost and died three blocks away from the rental agency.

Garrett and she had pushed it out of the intersection to the curb, grabbed the map out of the car, and hurried to the agency.

The only car that the put-upon man behind the counter had left was a two-door subcompact. "There's a convention in town. Every car and every room is booked. You're lucky I have this," he told them as he took Garrett's card and ran it through the machine.

Garrett didn't exactly see it as lucky. He circled the only vehicle on the lot, as if hoping that another view might somehow improve things. It didn't. The car looked small from every angle.

"It's a clown car." His last bit of patience evaporating, he threw up his hands. "How am I supposed to drive a clown car?"

Megan took the keys from his palm. "You don't," she said cheerfully. "I do. Get in on the passenger side and push the seat back as far as you can." She gave Garrett's torso a once-over. "Maybe that way there'll be enough room to accommodate those long legs of yours."

He scowled, but he had to admit that the suggestion made sense. They didn't have time for him to go scouting around to other rental agencies for another car. Besides, if what the man behind the counter said was true, there wasn't another car available, no matter where they went. For the time being, he was stuck.

He got in, his scowl deepening as he looked at her. He didn't like letting someone else drive. But he had no choice—something else he wasn't crazy about. Sitting on the driver's side would be torturous. "You're enjoying this, aren't you?"

"Absolutely." Buckling up, Megan opened the map she'd rescued from the other car and honed in on the Excelsior's major cross streets. Noting them, she flipped the map over her shoulder into the back seat. As she started the car, she began humming.

She didn't have to be so cheerful about this, he

thought. "Anyone ever tell you that you have some pretty annoying qualities?"

"More than once. Don't worry, you're in good company," she quipped, apparently enjoying the knowledge that she was getting under his skin.

He grew quiet for a moment, trying to sort through a barrage of feelings, most of which defied sorting. Garrett looked at her profile—and thought of last night. Any way you cut it, she was a beautiful woman. Why hadn't someone snapped her up by now? "Is that why you're not married?"

The question, coming out of nowhere, stunned Megan for a second. But it wasn't one she hadn't fielded before, usually from well-meaning acquaintances who couldn't understand her life-style. She gave him the answer she gave everyone, and didn't let herself wonder why he was asking.

"I'm not married because an FBI-special-agent-turned-private-investigator isn't at the top of most men's shopping list when it comes to a prospective lifelong mate."

"So it's your career choice that's kept you from finding someone to share your life with?"

She heard the skepticism in his voice. What was he after? "Yes," she bit off.

"Not your less than easygoing personality." It wasn't a question. He said the words slowly, as if digesting their meaning and impact.

He'd pushed her buttons again, she thought. How did he manage to keep finding them so easily? She glared at him before looking back at the road.

"You want 'less than easygoing'? I haven't *begun* to be less than easygoing, Wichita. Keep pushing my buttons," she warned, "and see what you get."

He'd rattled her. They were even. Garrett sat back. "Tempting as that offer is, I think I'll postpone it until after we wrap the case up."

Traffic was at a crawl. The rental clerk hadn't been kidding about that convention, she thought, annoyed. Riding the brake, she slanted a look at Garrett's smug face. He made it sound as if there was no definite end in sight.

"There is no 'after,' Wichita," she reminded him. "Once I locate Kathy and get her out of Velasquez's den of iniquity, that's it. I'm gone."

They both knew it was true, Garrett thought. Once she secured Kathy, she would be permanently out of his life. He had no idea why hearing it spoken out loud should irritate him as much as it did.

Maybe because *she* irritated him, he thought. Relentlessly.

Feeling as if there was a cramp forming in his left thigh, he tried to shift position and discovered that he couldn't—not without kicking a hole in the side of the car. Who were these cars made for, anyway?

"You're not getting Kathy out until after this goes down," he reminded her tersely. No matter what, there was no way he would allow her to mess up the operation. Not after all this time.

"We've been through this already—"

"I can have you restrained."

Megan bit her lower lip as she tried to contain her

exasperation. Experience had taught her that there were a great many things Wichita could do that fell into the recesses, the gray areas of the law. Things she instinctively knew he wouldn't hesitate to do if she got in his way. She was expendable. This crusade he'd undertaken was not.

The taste in her mouth was more bitter than it should have been. And that annoyed her. More than that, it worried her.

Her only recourse was bravado. Never wavering, she lobbed a shot over to his side. "And I can have things done to you that you can't even imagine."

Her tone was steely and ominous. For a moment, Garrett didn't know whether to believe her or not. He didn't know if *she* believed she was serious. "Are you threatening me?"

Her eyes were cold and unfathomable as she looked at him. "Only if you're threatening me."

He weighed his options and decided he didn't want to go to darker areas. Not yet. Annoyed at her, and at himself for being soft, he stared straight ahead at the dark sports car in front of them. "I don't have time for this."

"Good," she pronounced. "Then let's get on with it."

Traffic broke up a little about a mile later. Megan took it as a good omen. She drove up to the hotel, bypassing the dark-blue-jacketed valets and going to the self-parking structure.

Getting out, she rounded the hood and then stood

waiting at Garrett's side, amused. She bent over and peered in. She'd seen suspects being grilled who looked more comfortable. ''Need help getting out?''

''They should have supplied a can opener with it.''

As she watched him unfold his body, she tried very hard not to remember how that same body had felt against her last night. ''Not everyone can reach up and touch the sky.''

''I'm six-three, not nine foot eight.''

Megan looked indifferent to his protest. Pocketing the keys, she fell into step beside him as he walked to the hotel entrance. ''All right, we're here. Now what?''

''Now we wait.''

''Wait?'' The very sound of the word made her feel restless.

He walked ahead of her into the lobby, then slowed down until she was beside him.

''Until they make their move.'' Which was, unless things had changed, to be tomorrow night. He motioned her toward the rear of the lobby, where banks of elevators stood. ''The department has a suite just below theirs in the tower.''

He'd lengthened his stride again, and she hurried to keep up. ''The tower,'' she echoed. ''It sounds like something out of medieval history.''

''Some of it probably is,'' he said vaguely.

The next moment, one of the elevators arrived, its doors opening. Several people got in with them. The conversation was tabled until they got off on their floor. Megan could feel the tension rising with each passing floor.

There were two other DEA agents inside the suite below Velasquez's. They greeted Garrett and looked at Megan with blatant interest. Garrett introduced them as Harris and Langtree. Both were balding and in their late thirties or early forties. Neither was stocky or complacent. Megan thought they looked almost interchangeable.

She gathered by their expressions that they had already been filled in on her part in this, and seemed to be at ease with it.

Unlike Wichita.

His back toward her, he behaved as if he was completely oblivious to her presence. "Anything?" He looked from Harris to Langtree.

Harris, the shorter of the two, shook his head. He pointed with a set of chopsticks to emphasize his statement. There were containers of Chinese food littering one of the tables. "Nothing to distinguish them from any other gamblers making a long weekend out of it."

"Except that they're carting around an underage girl," Megan interjected. Both men turned to look at her. She took Kathy's photograph from her purse. "Did either of you see her?"

Langtree, who was closest to her, took the photograph and looked at it with interest, then passed it on to Harris. "Not me. You, Harris?"

Returning the photograph to her, Harris got back to his cold dinner. "They've got a few women with them upstairs, but nobody who looks like her."

Megan refused to give in to the panicky feeling that was attempting to take hold. Refused to believe that Kathy might have been abandoned somewhere along the way.

"Maybe I should take a look myself."

Garrett immediately turned on her. "Not possible."

"Calm down. I didn't mean go *up* there." She looked at the other two agents. "Don't you have any of those James-Bond-type gadgets planted in the suite? The ones that tell you how high a guy's blood pressure is if he's standing three feet away from the device?"

"Can't afford to plant anything in the suite," Garrett told her, his voice masking his frustration. If they could have planted bugs at least, then they would be ahead of the game, instead of waiting for Velasquez to make the first move. "If they detect something's wrong, it's all over."

"Great. All right, work with the basics," she implored Harris and Langtree. "Short, blond, thin…" She peered at one face, then the other for any signs of recognition.

"All of them are blond," Langtree told her. "He likes to surround himself with blondes."

Another idiosyncrasy, she thought. The man was enough to make a battery of psychiatrists rub their hands together in glee.

"How about short?" Garrett questioned. Megan shot him a surprised look. She would have expected him to be completely consumed by his own operation.

Harris paused to think, exchanging a glance with Langtree for confirmation before nodding. "One of them's shorter than the others, though she really looks older than your girl.'' The chopsticks pointed toward the photograph.

''Makeup,'' Megan answered, masking her nervousness with a silent prayer. *Please, let it be makeup.*

Trying to pull her thoughts together, she slid the photograph back into her purse and turned away from the men. In the background, she heard Garrett lower his voice as he talked to the other agents.

What if Kathy *wasn't* there? The thought, planted by Harris's doubts, nagged at her.

There was only one thing to do. She had to get in there—into the suite—to look around.

She already knew that Wichita wasn't going to like it. But she wasn't here to please Wichita. She was here to rescue Kathy and bring her home. Alive.

Taking care not to call attention to herself, Megan began to slip out of the room.

''Where are you going?''

She froze at the sound of Garrett's voice, but didn't turn around.

''The bathroom—if it's all right with you.'' Her voice was doused in sarcasm, and she heard one of the other men stifle a laugh.

''Whatever,'' Garrett muttered.

She'd flustered him, she thought with triumph. But a small part of her felt guilty for what she was about to do. She was going to embarrass him in front of his colleagues. And no man took that lightly.

It couldn't be helped, she told herself.

Once in the bathroom, she gave herself until the

count of ten, then opened the door again as silently as she could. There was just the hint of Garrett's shoulder visible from the other room. The murmur of voices carried, not clearly, but clearly enough for her to glean that they were exchanging information.

Closing the bathroom door again to make it appear as if she were still inside, Megan slipped out of the hotel suite.

Once in the hall, she lost no time running to the stairwell. Instead of going up, she went down a flight, hoping to buy herself a little time, in case Wichita went looking for her too soon.

Somewhere, she thought, on one of these floors, there had to be a cleaning cart. And a maid who could use a little extra money.

The hotel had twenty floors. Megan went through almost half of them before she finally found what she was looking for. Ten minutes later, Megan—a kerchief tied around her head to hide her hair and wearing a uniform more than a size too large for her—got off on the floor above the DEA suite.

It didn't matter that she was a former FBI special agent, or that she was trained to keep a cool, clear head in these situations. She was human, and the pads on her fingertips were damp.

She focused on Kathy—and nothing else.

"Housekeeping!" Megan called out in a singsong voice as she inserted the card into the tower suite's lock and pulled it out again.

She would have preferred entering far more quietly,

but without the benefit of a camera in the suite, she didn't know if there was anyone near the door. To enter without announcing herself would have been too suspicious. At least this way, she had a chance of seeing Kathy.

If the girl was here.

Megan pushed the cart in front of her, wishing it was a little taller, or that, for once in her life, she was a little shorter.

She barely got three feet into the suite. A hulking, angry-looking man quickly confronted her, blocking her way. It would have been easier blasting her way through a brick wall.

"Nobody sent for you."

She looked at him blankly, as if the words had no meaning to her. "My job," she said to him in halting English. "I do my job. I clean, make beds, yes?"

With a quick movement, she circumvented him and managed to get the cart as far as the center of the front room. Just beyond, she saw an open door. The layout was identical to that of the floor below, making that a bedroom. She caught a glimpse of several women inside—young girls, by the sound of their voices. Shifting the cart, Megan tried to reach the room to get a better look.

"No."

The man grabbed her arm roughly, pulling her back. His fingers dug into her flesh. Her immediate instincts summoned moves that her training had made second nature. She struggled to keep them at bay—housekeeping maids were not trained in tae kwan do.

"Nobody wants the rooms cleaned now—understand?" he barked into her face.

Just then, one of the girls came to the doorway, drawn by the commotion. Her eyes were fearful as they darted from the man to the woman he was holding.

Recognition was instant, despite the sophisticated dress and makeup.

Kathy.

"What's going on?" the girl stammered.

"Nothing, get back inside," the man ordered Kathy and the two other girls who were standing behind her.

Another man came from the recesses of yet another bedroom. Dressed in a white shirt and white slacks, Jorge Velasquez's face momentarily appeared to be darker than it was. There were sharp creases about his nose and mouth, pressed in by the sun. The smile on his lips had an edgy, dangerous feel to it. Megan watched him look her over.

"What's going on?"

The hulk jerked one thumb at her, still holding her wrist with the other hand. "She came in. Says she wants to clean." He fairly snarled the explanation.

Velasquez came closer, as other men entered the front room. Megan saw eight in all.

"Don't be so hard on her. She's only doing her job." Velasquez imitated her singsong voice as he said the word. Then his smile widened to show perfectly straight, perfectly white teeth. "Right, honey?"

Maintaining the blank look in her eyes, Megan

smiled innocently at him. She bobbed her head up and down. "Yes, job."

Velasquez laughed, entertained. Taking out a thick wad of money, he peeled off a bill from the top, as careless with the hundred as another man might be with a quarter. He stuffed the bill into her pocket.

"Here, come back later. There's nothing to clean now." He turned to the man who still held her wrist. "See her out and treat her with respect," he cautioned. "My mother was a cleaning lady."

Behind her, she heard one of the girls moan. Two of the men in the background were herding the girls back into the bedroom.

Megan's heart quickened as she was forcibly escorted out. She looked over her shoulder, fighting the urge to push the cart into the bodyguard and run back to grab Kathy. But she knew she wouldn't get more than two feet before she was brought down.

"Someone sick?" Eyes wide, she looked at the man beside her.

"Not your concern," the bodyguard snapped, and pushed her out. The door slammed shut behind her.

Kathy was alive! That was all that mattered right now. Kathy was alive, and she was going to get her out of there.

Adrenaline pumped through her, doing double-time. It continued even after the elevator arrived and she stepped inside. Megan held her breath until the doors finally closed.

But they opened again one floor below. And before his image fully registered, Garrett was reaching in for her. Grabbing her wrist, he yanked her out of the elevator. Megan just barely managed to pull the cart out with her.

There was unbridled fury in his eyes.

"What the hell are you trying to do—get yourself killed?" It was all he could do to keep from shouting in her face. Holding firmly onto her arm, he dragged her over to the suite. Garret jammed the card into the lock, then pulled it out and pushed open the door. He shoved Megan into the room ahead of him, struggling to keep from shaking her apart. He figured she should be counting herself lucky that he wasn't strangling her there and then. He certainly wanted to.

Megan pulled her arm free, giving no indication that his hard grip had hurt her. She'd braved the enemy camp and survived. She could face him down, too.

"It's called surveillance work," she retorted.

"It's called stupidity. Harris and Langtree already did the surveillance—"

"They couldn't tell me if Kathy was there," she snapped back, cutting him short. "I wanted to see for myself. I needed to know she was alive."

Alive? he thought. Did she have any idea how close she came to not being alive herself?

"If they'd made you, you wouldn't be rescuing anybody. You'd be coming home in so many pieces they'd be too small to qualify as a jigsaw puzzle." He'd seen what Velasquez did with law enforcement officers, and it was the stuff nightmares were made of. "My God, woman, do you realize who those people are? You cross them, there is no forwarding address for your mail. Ever. Do I make myself clear?''

Megan swallowed, fighting not to be intimidated by Wichita's anger. She didn't deceive herself into believing that it had anything to do with her safety. He cared only about the safety of the operation.

She dragged the kerchief off her head, and tossed her hair. "How did you know where I was? I thought you said that you can't risk bugging Velasquez's suite."

"We can't. But we've got cameras planted on the floor by both elevator banks. After I discovered that you pulled a disappearing act, I saw you on the camera, getting out of the elevator."

She glanced at the monitor. All that was evident now was the empty hallway. Megan looked down at the kerchief in her hand. "How did you know it was me?"

"I knew." He didn't add that he would have recognized her anywhere. That when he realized she'd slipped out of the bathroom and was probably in the process of doing something like this, his heart had all but stopped. That would be giving her too much of an advantage over him. "Now are you going to stay put, or do I have to tie you up?"

"I can't stay put," she protested. "There's a maid on the tenth floor waiting for me to return her cart and her uniform."

He indicated the door. "All right, let's go."

Megan looked at him. What was he up to? "You're coming with me?"

How could she possibly think otherwise, after what she'd just pulled? he thought. "Damn straight, I am. I'm not letting you out of my sight again until this goes down."

There were a lot of hours from now until then. "What if I really have to go to the bathroom?" The question was baiting him, and she knew it, but she couldn't resist asking.

His look was steely and left no room for mercy. "You'll hold it."

Megan stared at him in disbelief. "Until tomorrow night?"

Until a week from now—if it took that. "You should have thought of that before."

"What are you so angry about?" she demanded. "I wasn't going to ruin your operation."

"And you're not going to get a chance to," he informed her tersely. "Now let's go find this maid so you can give her back her clothes."

What he didn't add was that it wasn't the operation he was worried about. It was the thought of her being killed that made his blood run cold.

Chapter 14

Megan rapped twice on the utility closet door, then stood back as it opened a crack. She smiled encouragingly at the woman who looked at her with large brown eyes. "I'm back, just like I promised."

The woman looked enormously relieved.

"Be right back," Megan tossed over her shoulder at Garrett before shutting the door behind her.

Despite the fact that she'd just disappeared into a utility closet, Garrett considered checking it out for another possible exit. He wouldn't put anything past Megan.

Folding his arms before him, he leaned against the wall and waited. He didn't need this sort of aggravation, he told himself. At this point in his life, he wasn't sure exactly what it was that he did need, but it didn't include constantly being challenged, constantly having to be on his toes—because of a woman. That was guaranteed to wear him out before his time.

As he waited, his thoughts began to stray again. Garrett smiled, then sobered when he realized what he was doing.

When the door opened again, Megan walked out first. Following in her wake was the maid, who looked at Garrett nervously. Megan caught the woman's wary expression.

"Don't mind him, he scares everyone. Here." She pressed the hundred dollars that Velasquez had given her into the woman's hand. "This is yours."

The woman looked down at the bill uncertainly. All signs of wariness faded a moment later. Her smile was wide, electric.

"Thank you, miss," she said haltingly.

Garrett caught a glimpse of the bill's denomination before it disappeared into the maid's pocket. Taking Megan's arm, he ushered her away from the closet and toward the elevator. The sooner he got her back upstairs, the better he would feel.

"Is that the going rate for borrowed uniforms and carts these days?" Leaning over her, he pressed the button for the elevator.

Megan felt his arm brush against her chest. It was enough to stir memories. She shut them away. There was no place for them in her life. "I already paid her. That was what Velasquez slipped into my hand before I left."

"What?" He looked at her sharply. "You spoke to Velasquez?"

She couldn't put a name to the emotion behind his tone, and it made her uneasy.

"He spoke to me—as the maid," she emphasized, in case Garrett thought she'd blown the operation. "Said his mother had been a cleaning lady." She shrugged, looking up over the elevator bank to watch the progression of numbers. The closest car was five floors away. "Maybe he felt guilty."

That would be the day, thought Garrett. "The man doesn't *feel* anything. He doesn't have a humane bone in his body. Maybe he just liked being a big shot," Garrett contradicted.

"Maybe," she agreed.

She didn't feel like getting into an argument with him over the dealer's motives. That was the least of her concerns. She was still frustrated that she hadn't been able to get Kathy out of the suite.

"How did you talk the maid into that?" Garrett wanted to know. "This kind of thing only happens in movies."

"Life imitates art," she answered glibly. The elevator finally arrived—empty. Megan stepped in ahead of him. "Besides, money does go a long way in convincing people to do things. I told her that I wanted to play a joke on my fiancé."

Garrett pressed for their floor. "And she believed you?"

It was evident to Megan by his expression that Garrett wouldn't believe anyone.

"I have an honest face." She raised her chin and pasted on a broad smile.

Garrett laughed shortly. "Only if you stretch the concept."

The elevator stopped on the next floor, and a tourist family walked in. The conversation was put on hold.

Getting off on their floor, Garrett took her arm and marshaled her down the hall.

"I can walk," she protested.

"You can also run," he countered tersely. Opening the door, he ushered her in before him.

Megan looked around. Harris and Langtree were gone.

"Where are your friends?"

"Busy." The less she knew, the better off everyone would be—including her. Garrett saw the annoyed look in her eyes. "You want an agent-by-agent rundown?"

She waved the sarcasm away. She didn't care what they were up to, as long as in the end she got Kathy out safely.

Restless, Megan moved around the suite. Each time she entered one of the other rooms, Garrett shadowed her movements, staying close behind. Exactly what did he expect her to do—disappear into thin air?

Hands on hips, she swung around and confronted him. "You're not really serious about not letting me out of your sight, are you?"

"Never more serious about anything in my life," he said mildly.

She saw that he had picked up one of the take-out containers and was eating from it. It had to be stone-cold by now.

Seeing her eye the container, Garrett held it out to her. "Hungry?"

She was too keyed up to think about eating. "What is it you think I'm going to do?"

"I don't know." He followed her back into the front room. "I don't know what you're capable of, Megan. I didn't think you'd actually go waltzing into their suite, but you did." Finished with the container, he set it down on the coffee table with the others. "It's better for everyone all around if I just keep you close."

The uneasiness she'd been feeling began to grow, feeding on things that had no name, no form. On memories of a night that was best forgotten by both parties involved. "How close?"

Slowly, a smile curved his mouth as he looked down at her. The lectures, the reprimands, the anger—all faded. "That all depends."

A smart person would have known enough to retreat. And Megan had always considered herself smart. But maybe not tonight. Tonight she was also inexplicably fascinated by this man who refused to be pigeonholed. "On what?"

By now, there wasn't enough room between their bodies to wedge a paper cut. "On you."

Megan found that she was having trouble swallowing. She was an idiot—there was no other word for it. A certified, addle-brained idiot. She knew exactly where this was going.

Exactly where she wanted it to go, without actually acknowledging the fact to herself.

But she had never been one to just drift along with the tide, never been one to allow things to sweep her away. She'd always made choices, cold hard choices. Even if she didn't admit it to herself at the time.

There were no accidents in Megan Andreini's life.

She wanted to be here, in this room, with this man.

He held his breath, waiting for her answer, for some indication that she wanted this as much as he did.

Megan glanced toward the door. There was no one here now, but that could change at any moment. She didn't relish the idea of someone walking in on them.

"Doesn't it depend on your friends?" she asked pointedly.

His mouth curved a little more, teasing her. Making her pulse flutter. He shook his head in response to her question. "I'm not into things like that."

He *would* give that meaning to her words, she thought, just to rattle her. She frowned slightly. "I mean—when are they coming back."

"They're not coming back." He saw the surprised look in her eyes. "At least, not until the morning. They pulled a different detail."

She looked at him knowingly. "How convenient." A thrill passed over her.

They both knew he was in charge of the case. "Just efficient, that's all."

God, but Garrett wanted to kiss her. To hold her and feel her against him again. He should have been thinking of the operation, of what was at stake, but all he could think of was her.

Garrett placated his conscience with the fact that

everything was in place. The drop wasn't scheduled to happen until tomorrow night, and there were agents everywhere in the city, alert and watching the drop site, as well as all possible exits to and from the hotel.

With that many eyes watching, it was all right if his were distracted for a few minutes, feasting on something else.

She cocked her head, studying his face. The man could twist words with the best of them. She had to remember that, and not allow herself to get carried away.

But when he touched her shoulders, resting just the pads of his palms on them, she had trouble breathing normally.

"Is that what this is going to be?" She searched his face for a sign. "Efficient?"

"There is no name for what this is going to be, Megan," he told her.

Because what Garrett felt right now had no name— none that he was willing to ascribe to it. It wasn't lust, because he'd known lust: hot, flashing and then gone. And it wasn't desire—at least, not only desire. Desire consumed whatever it touched until the moment it was sated. But there had been no satiety—not with her. There had only been a need for more, even in the wake of complete exhaustion.

Something like that had no name. It just was.

"No name, huh?" Her eyes smiled. He was just as lost in this as she was. Knowing that helped. The next moment, her breath caught in her throat again as he began undoing the buttons on her blouse. "Sounds as if we're on the brink of some scientific discovery."

His eyes on hers, Garrett continued working away the buttons, undressing her. "Maybe we are."

Excitement drummed urgent fingers through her, urging her to action. She hurried through two of his buttons, then undid one for each one of hers that he worked free.

When he drew the sleeves down her arms, she mimicked the movements with his shirt. The two articles of clothing tangled as they fell to the floor together.

"Think they'll name it after us?" she asked, her voice low, desire throbbing deep in her throat. "They always name things after the people who discover them." Megan bit her lip as she felt his hands on her hips, urging her skirt down a few inches at a time before slipping in. Goose bumps formed instantly as she felt his warm flesh touch hers.

"Then we'll have to argue over whose name comes first." He drew his breath in as he felt her fingers slide the zipper of his slacks down, then press ever so slightly along his body. Along his growing desire for her.

The woman looked like an angel and had the soul of an old-world courtesan.

What was worse, he realized, though he was unable to do anything about it, was that she had his number—down to the last digit.

"We don't have to argue," she whispered, pressing her lips to his throat.

The taste of his pulse jumping beneath her mouth lit a torch to her excitement.

"How would you like to settle it?" he asked with effort.

With a flick of his thumb and forefinger, the hook on her white bra came undone. He looked down to watch. The fabric hovered along her skin, held there by memory, before it drifted away as well. He cupped her breasts in his hands, his fingers slowly caressing her.

Garrett felt Megan's smile against his cheek. "Two throws out of three?" she proposed.

The feel of her fingers—gently moving, touching, skimming, dipping low beneath his briefs before she drew them away altogether—threatened to bring him to his knees.

Breathing as hard as if he'd just run a mile to establish a new world record, Garrett caught her wrists. He raised her hands over her head, bringing her breasts up tantalizingly high against his chest.

In a heartbeat, he was the prisoner—not she.

The slight brush of her nipples along his skin was exquisite agony. He fought to keep from devouring her here and now. They had the night before them, he reminded himself, and he knew it would be their last. He wanted to savor it—to savor her—for as long as it was mortally possible.

With every movement, every breath, she undid him a little more. He'd never known anyone like her, never dreamed anyone could brand him so indelibly.

He kissed her eyes, her mouth, her cheeks. "Show

me what you have,'' he urged, his breath enflaming her.

The effort to keep her mind on what he was saying and not what he was doing was a losing battle. ''I thought I was.''

''More,'' Garrett prompted urgently against her neck, feathering light, teasing kisses along her jawline. ''Show me more.''

He wanted to taste her passion, feel her desire. He wanted Megan to give him what she'd never given anyone else.

Megan almost sank down then, her legs turning to liquid as the heat of his body melted hers. In an effort to bring him down with her, she slanted her mouth against his, her hands fisting in his hair, her body sealing itself to his.

It frightened her that she wanted him more than she'd ever wanted anyone, anything. It frightened her that she was powerless to shut off this need, this desire. That she was powerless to turn away from it, even though nothing could ever come of it.

But for now, there was nothing else—only Garrett. Garrett and the fiery passion that he aroused within her. A fiery passion that she had not known had existed before he entered her life.

Unable to hold back, unwilling to even try, she peaked the moment his fingers dipped between her legs, and twisted against him as she tried to absorb the feeling deep into her core. She twisted more as she tried to absorb the feel of his hand along her body.

The feel of him.

He wanted all of her at his mercy, for he was completely at hers. At the mercy of a woman who had no idea of the kind of power she held over him. Seeking to imprison her, he'd managed to slam the bars on himself as well. He was in this cage with her, held fast by a desire that was so large, so unwieldy and untamable, that it felt lethal.

It wasn't in his nature to be imprisoned. He had always sought to escape and to remain free—no matter what the price.

But his nature changed that evening. And whatever it became, he set it in her hands, to do with what she would. As long as she made love with him. As long as he could feel her lips racing along his body. As long as he could taste her body in kind.

He sold his soul to her.

Over and over again, he took her, bringing Megan from peak to fantastic peak, assaulting her with his tongue, his lips, his hands. His eyes.

Making her feel beautiful.

Making her feel.

Hot, panting, and still so desperately needy, Megan pulled Garrett down to her, afraid that she would expire before he joined with her. Her eyes were cloudy as she looked up at him. "Does this place come with a fire extinguisher?" Every inch of her was on fire, deliciously, wantonly on fire. If she could choose the moment that she was to leave this world, it would be after a night like tonight.

Framing her face in his hands, he kissed her before answering. Then, because one kiss fed on another, he kissed her again until he could hardly form his question. "Why?"

"Because I think we're going to need it, Wichita."

With her body outlined by sheets that were already hopelessly tangled, Garrett shifted his body over her. He threaded his fingers through hers, his eyes hazy with feelings, his body barely restrained from taking the final moment. "Garrett."

She didn't understand. "What?"

"Call me Garrett," he told her. "I want to hear you say my name."

Megan's chin lifted stubbornly, but there was mischief in her eyes as she held her ground. "Let's not get personal, here."

He kissed first one corner of her mouth, then the other, before his lips surrounded her chin, sucking gently, bringing it down again. "Say it."

Megan opened her lips, as if to acquiesce, then she raised her head quickly, capturing his mouth. Capturing the moment.

His protest died as he felt her open for him, taking him into her. There was no room for argument, for protests. There was only room for the exquisite excitement that came of their joining.

Sealed together, they took the moment and each other, shuddering as the final explosion racked their bodies in unison.

When it was over, and when the pleasure receded into something that was less overwhelming, Garrett held her to him tightly, swearing to himself that all he felt was physical and that he could take it or leave it—and her—at will.

Cursing her for the lie he was telling himself.

Holding her close and drawing in the beating of her heart against his.

Damn, when had life gotten so complicated?

Very slowly, his breathing returned to normal, bringing with it his pulse and, belatedly, his senses. With a sigh, Garrett shifted onto his elbows, pulling his body away from hers.

Megan felt the chill instantly but told herself she didn't. That it was only the air against her skin and nothing more. She reached for the sheet and drew it over her. It didn't help.

Garrett looked at her for a long moment. Even in the supposed throes of passion, she'd defied him, unable to do something as simple as saying his name when he'd asked. Her refusal irked him. And it shouldn't have.

"You have got to be the most stubborn woman I ever met."

She knew exactly what he was referring to. And she had her own reasons for not giving in. "Why, because I don't take instructions during lovemaking?"

There was no explaining what was in his heart—why Megan's refusal rankled him the way it did. He couldn't even form the words satisfactorily in his own mind.

He took a deep breath, looking away. "Something like that," he muttered.

Megan wanted to tell him. She wanted to let him

know that he had touched something. Something that made her afraid. Something that had been so paralyzed within her that she had believed it was gone altogether. She wanted to let him know that calling him by his first name, no matter how insignificant it might sound, would let him completely into her world and give him a powerful hold over her.

But she couldn't explain. The words wouldn't come, because the words would make her weak. A target for pain. She refused to be a target.

And yet, there was something in his eyes. Something that wouldn't let her turn away, either. Torn, confused, she touched his shoulder.

"What?"

Megan nearly turned away then, but that would have been the safer thing to do. So, because it had always been the way she'd lived her life, she ventured out onto the tightrope, if only for a second. If only for a view.

"If it could be anyone," she confessed enigmatically, "it would be you."

He looked into her eyes and understood. But knew, too, that she needed the cloak of ambiguity in order to survive the words, the feeling. "Bureau teach you to talk in code?"

She smiled then. "Bureau taught me never to lead with my chin."

"This chin?" He nibbled on it.

Desire sprang up from a hidden well, refreshed. Eager. Wanting.

"Yes," she said with difficulty.

"Just wanted to get my bearings straight."

His lips moved to her ear, his breath sending shivers through her. She felt his desire growing as she heard his breath shorten.

She drew his hands to her breasts. "You're always forgetting your map," she reminded him.

He rubbed his thumb along her hardening tips. "That's because real men don't need directions on how to get somewhere. They just know."

There was no question in her mind, as she arched into him, that he was just that. A real man.

Chapter 15

"Okay, this is it, everybody. We're on!" Garrett gave the order to mobilize into the walkie-talkie he was holding.

On the monitor in front of him, Velasquez and his men were walking out of the suite one floor above. After an entire day of inertia, things were finally beginning to move.

"About time," Harris responded on the other end.

It was, Garrett thought as he watched the men leave the suite. Way past time. If they pulled this off and arrested Velasquez with the goods, the drug dealer's fall was fifteen years overdue. The last five years had been spent trying to set a trap that would catch not only the little fish, but the bigger one as well. Until now, Velasquez had always managed to elude them at the last minute.

Not this time, Garrett swore to himself.

Overconfidence, he reasoned, had made the drug dealer careless about the little details. And it was the little details that always tripped them up.

Garrett could feel it in his bones. Tonight was the night that Andy, and all the others who had succumbed to the lure of the drugs Velasquez pushed, would finally have their revenge.

Switching off the walkie-talkie so he could talk to her in private, Garrett turned toward Megan. There was no time to dwell on the last twelve hours. No time to relive any of the moments they'd spent in each other's arms, keeping not only boredom at bay, but time and thought as well.

There was only enough time to issue a terse warning.

"I want you to be careful." His eyes narrowed as he saw her chin rise. He was beginning to know the signs. "And don't give me any of your invincible-woman garbage, understand? You can get shot just like everyone else. Once they're all out, give it ten minutes and then go get Kathy. There should only be one man left."

A movement on the screen drew Megan's attention back to the monitor.

"I don't think that's possible." Megan set her mouth grimly as she pointed to the monitor. One of Velasquez's men was herding Kathy out before him. "Why would he take her?" There wasn't going to be any need for a courier. "What do you think it means?"

From the information the DEA had gathered, Kathy Teasdale was the newest member of Velasquez's inner circle. Her parents were easily the wealthiest; Velasquez had to know that.

This had the smell of ransom about it. Garrett didn't like it. ''It means that he thinks something's up. She's his insurance.''

The last man out closed the door. By Megan's count, that only left one man in the suite with the other three girls—just as Garrett had speculated.

''Insurance against what?''

''Us.'' It was the only logical assumption. ''Maybe he thinks the DEA knows.''

That didn't make sense to her. Velasquez had already called off the exchange twice. ''But then why go through with it at all? Why not just switch to another location again?''

''His supplier's getting irritated with this game of musical cities, and Velasquez isn't sure whether we know or not. Besides, word has it his supply's drying up, and he needs this to stay in business.'' Frustrated by this added complication, Garrett threw up his hands. ''Look, if I could second-guess him, he'd be ours by now.''

Curbing his temper, Garrett switched the walkie-talkie on again. ''All units, Velasquez has a young girl with him. Looks like she's a hostage. Exercise caution. We'd like to get her out alive if possible.''

If possible.

The phrase leaped out at Megan and burned itself

into her brain. She placed a hand on the walkie-talkie. "*Make* it possible," she ordered.

He drew the walkie-talkie away, switching it off. "I'll do what I can, Megan. It's the best I can promise."

When Garrett started for the door, she fell into place beside him. "Looks like we're riding together to the end on this one."

Garrett stopped dead. "Megan—"

"Don't 'Megan' me," she cautioned. There was no room for debate, and no time. "I go with you or behind you—but I go, understand?"

He understood, all right. Understood that the woman was pigheaded beyond belief. "She's a client, Megan. There's no reason to put your life on the line—"

Megan knew he didn't believe it for a minute. "She's a fourteen-year-old girl, and probably scared out of her mind. If she were Andy—?"

She didn't have to finish.

Exasperated, Garrett waved her forward. It was either that, he thought, or lock her in the closet. He had to admit that, for a split second, he entertained the latter solution and found more than a little pleasure in the image.

"C'mon, we're running out of time."

Megan pulled the seat belt tightly around her. "Do you know where we're going?"

Garrett was once more in the driver's seat. The department had secured a vehicle for him that accommodated his long frame, and the subcompact had been returned to the rental agency by another operative with far less field experience.

Garrett slanted an icy look in her direction. This time, he'd made sure he double-checked directions before starting out. This was far too important for him to risk getting tripped up by even the slightest detail.

"Yes, I know where we're going. It's a private airstrip just outside Reno. The drugs are coming in via a private jet that belongs to a very prominent socialite who finds running on the wrong side of the law a great way to get thrills."

He'd hoped that Visalia, the Colombian drug lord who was on the other end of this exchange, would come along, but the man had wisely opted to send someone else in his place.

Some other time, Garrett promised himself silently.

"We can't get our hands on the main supplier—he's still in Colombia somewhere. But we can break off a few of his tentacles. And we can nail Velasquez." The last was said with relish.

The lights of the city were behind them. Megan looked out on the darkening road, wondering what was going through Kathy's mind. Was she scared? Had she lost all hope of seeing her parents again? With effort, Megan put the questions aside.

"Isn't that rather ironic?" she asked. She saw him raise a brow. "Velasquez going to an airport when he's afraid of flying?"

He shrugged. "He's not looking to fly the plane.

He's looking to get richer from its cargo. I don't know about ironic, but I do know this is way overdue."

She could smell the tension in the air. Adrenaline began building within her. She saw nothing ahead but the road, made brighter by the twin beams coming from Garrett's headlights.

"You're sure your men are on the scene?"

"In every conceivable position," he assured her. With a day's warning, they'd been able to infiltrate the area. "And one of our operatives is even an attendant on the incoming flight. That's how we knew where and when."

"You've got everything covered, then." She tried to calm the edgy feeling that was starting to build within her.

"Nothing is ever covered," he told her, voicing her own sentiments. She saw Garrett's hands tighten on the steering wheel. "Velasquez was in our grasp two years ago and managed to wiggle through. We couldn't capture him. As always, Velasquez got away, and someone else took the fall."

She heard the barely controlled anger in his voice. "You'll get him."

The simple prophesy made him smile. "Optimism? Coming from you?"

"Not optimism—just fact," she countered. "You're too good at what you do not to bring him down eventually." And when he did, she thought, then what? "What are you going to do afterwards?"

"Afterwards?" Garrett wasn't sure what she was getting at.

Megan nodded, looking straight ahead. She didn't want him to realize just how interested she was in his answer. "After Velasquez ceases to be the driving force in your life."

Garrett didn't care for the way that sounded, or the way she said it. But he would have been less than honest with himself if he didn't admit that it was true. Bringing Velasquez to justice had been his only focus for a great deal of his adulthood. Once that was accomplished, hard as it was to realize, there would be a hole in his life.

But, "I haven't given it much thought," was all he said to her.

Megan believed him. He hadn't thought about the fact that capturing Velasquez would be the first step toward his leading a normal life, or that he could finally begin to heal.

She said nothing. She'd come as close to asking Garrett about their future—his and hers—as she was going to. If he couldn't take the hint, then she wasn't going to push it.

A mile away from the airstrip, Garrett turned off the car's headlights. Afraid that one of Velasquez's people might have stumbled onto their frequency, the walkie-talkies were dormant. Communication was limited to watching tracking blips on a portable computer's screen. The blips, Garrett told Megan, represented his agents' positions around the airport.

She was familiar with the program. "If you can have this," she whispered to him, "can't Velasquez?"

"Not with our modifications," he assured her. "It's too technical to explain."

But computers were her passion as well as her field of expertise. "Try me," she encouraged.

They heard the roar of a duel-engine plane in the distance. He stopped the car. "That would be the delivery. I'll have to explain it to you some other time."

Some other time. It was a throwaway phrase, yet, in her heart, she wanted to believe that he had said it in good faith. That there was to be a "some other time" for them.

Annoyed that she was allowing herself to be distracted, Megan got out of the car and focused on the area around them.

The airstrip was just up ahead, and on it a hangar that housed a handful of private airplanes belonging to the area's wealthy vacationers. Megan wondered how many of Garrett's people were on the premises, and if they would be enough.

It didn't take much to figure out that Velasquez had chosen the airstrip for the exchange because it was so isolated and seemed to eliminate the possibility of a surprise attack. But by the same token, there was nowhere for him and his men to flee if an attack managed to be launched.

At least, Megan thought, moving behind Garrett through the high foliage, it sounded good in theory.

Aside from the plane that was coming into view and the two limousines waiting for it on the ground, she didn't see anyone. "Where are your people?"

"There," he assured her.

She hoped that he wasn't bluffing.

Surrounded by his people, Velasquez kept a tight human wall around him. And right before him, like a talisman with which he mocked them, was Kathy.

Joining Harris and Langtree on the far end of the hangar, Megan took the long-range binoculars that Harris offered her. On the ground, bound, gagged and unconscious, was one of the two sentries that Velasquez had posted on this side of the hangar. The other, Langtree had told Garrett, had been "taken care of."

Megan trained the binoculars on Kathy. The girl looked terrified. "That bastard's handcuffed to her," Megan realized. She lowered the binoculars and looked at Garrett. "What's he trying to do?"

"Stay alive."

There was no way that this was going to go down without gunfire. And that worried Garrett. Always before, he'd been able to hone in on the activity alone. His agents were all able-bodied, each capable of taking care of himself. But he'd brought an unknown into this mix. He'd brought Megan, whom he'd never watched under fire. Whom he didn't want to see under fire.

Having her here interfered with his concentration.

As the plane touched down not far from the limousines, Velasquez and his people began to walk toward it. The engines grew silent.

Show time, thought Garrett.

"You stay here," Garrett ordered Megan. Before she could protest, he was walking toward the other end of the hangar—and Velasquez. Garrett unholstered his gun, aiming it toward the drug dealer. "This is the DEA," he announced. "You're all under arrest. Surrender your weapons." Instantly, men began to scramble out of cover, moving into the open, around the men by the limousines. "Otherwise, you won't get off this field alive."

Velasquez's response was to open fire. Gunfire echoed in the midnight air, mingling with the sounds of screams coming from Kathy and the woman who had just gotten off the plane. The socialite seemed to suddenly realize the penalty for dabbling on the dark side; panicked, she raced back into the plane.

Taking out her own weapon, Megan zigzagged to Garrett as the latter sought cover behind a plane. "Is that how it's done?" Her flippant tone camouflaged the slight quaver in her voice. When the first shot rang out, she'd thought that he'd been hit.

"I told you to stay back," he growled at her.

"I don't work for you, Wichita, remember?" Pressing against the side of the plane, she saved her ammunition. She couldn't hit anything from this distance. "How are we going to get Kathy away from him?"

"We're going to have to bring him down. It's the only way. There's too much blood on his hands—he's not about to allow her to walk." They heard the sound of an engine starting up, and he remembered the socialite. "Damn it, she's going to try to take off. Langtree!" he called over to the man. "Can you hit the fuel tank?"

It was only then that Megan realized the other agent had a rifle in his hand.

"I can try!" the man called back.

More rounds were exchanged. The plane began taxiing.

"McKenna, get one of your men in there with a car!" he shouted. "Block the pilot's way. If he can't taxi, he can't fly."

"What are you doing?" Megan demanded, trying to grab Garrett's arm as he left the cover of the plane.

"Taking a calculated risk." He shook her off. "Velasquez!" Garrett called out calmly, raising his voice above the sound of the engine. "You and your men can still walk off this field alive. Hand over your weapons. Anything is better than death."

The fool was going to walk right in front of Velasquez, Megan thought, her heart pounding. The next minute, she was hurrying after him, refusing to think her actions through. There wasn't time.

"All right, you've made your point," Velasquez allowed amiably.

From where Megan stood, she saw that the man had edged his way closer to the plane. He could sprint to it from where he was. When faced with being taken prisoner, fear of flying apparently took a back seat. She kept her eyes on him, afraid to even blink.

"No use dying here tonight. Not when there is so much to live for." He glanced toward the men around him. "You heard the man—put down your weapons."

"Too easy," Garrett murmured loudly enough for only Megan to hear.

But slowly, as the clatter of weapons being thrown

down was heard, men began moving forward, their hands raised.

Garrett walked over to Velasquez. Well dressed, with an acquired air of refinement, he hardly looked as if he were responsible for so much misery. But he was. And underneath the fine manners and finer clothes was the heart of a jackal. "You, too, Velasquez, raise your hands."

"I am handcuffed to this lovely girl," Velasquez protested, holding his hand up and pointing to the link. Kathy whimpered. "The keys—they are in my pocket." Velasquez's smile widened as he looked at Garrett. "With your permission?"

"You have to think I'm a fool."

But even as Garrett moved closer to the other man to get the keys himself, Velasquez pulled out his gun.

Seeing the glint of the gun barrel, Megan hurled herself at Velasquez, grabbing for his arm. Two shots, going wild, went off in quick succession, before he pulled his hand free, turning his weapon on Megan.

A silent cry stuck in her throat as Megan realized that she was looking down the barrel of a custom-made handgun.

A shot rang out, ricocheting in her ears.

Adrenaline screaming through her, Megan felt nothing. Before her, she saw Velasquez's eyes widened in stunned disbelief as he looked down at his chest. Blood poured out, soaking through his white shirt and onto his white jacket.

He fell forward, dragging Kathy down with him.

"That one's for Andy," Garrett said, his voice hardly above a whisper.

Kathy was shaking and sobbing hysterically, trying to get away but trapped by the handcuffs. As quickly as she could, Megan found the keys in Velasquez's pocket and uncuffed the girl from the dead man.

Once on her feet, Megan took Kathy into her arms. "It's okay, it's all over." Trying to calm her down, Megan stroked the girl's hair. "Shh. You're safe now. Wichita—"

She turned toward Garrett, only to see that there was an odd expression on his face. Still holding Kathy to her with one arm, she reached over to touch Garrett. She never got the chance to ask him what was wrong.

His eyes closed as he sank to his knees.

It was only then that Megan realized Velasquez's bullets had not gone far astray of their original target. Garrett had been shot twice.

She tried to catch him, but couldn't. The weight of his body brought Megan down to the ground with him.

"Omigod, you've been hit!" She bit back a panicky sob.

Garrett struggled to remain conscious. "What was your first clue?" The words dribbled out weakly.

"Harris!" she screamed, fighting not to let panic turn her mind blank.

There was commotion all around them. Someone had gone into the plane and was bringing out the socialite and the pilot. The other woman on the plane— the DEA agent—was wounded, but alive. None of that mattered. Nothing mattered but the man whose head she cradled on her blood-splattered lap.

"Harris, Wichita's been shot!" She looked down at Garrett's face, her heart freezing within her breast. There was blood everywhere. She couldn't even tell where the bullets had entered. "You'll be all right," she told Garrett fiercely. "Hang in there, you hear me?" She looked up again, searching for the familiar face amid those she didn't recognize. "Harris, call an ambulance!" she ordered. "Wichita's bleeding all over the place."

She was vaguely aware of someone sobbing in the background. It had to be Kathy, Megan thought numbly, even as she felt tears sliding down her cheeks.

Stripping off her jacket, she balled it up and pressed it against one of the holes she finally saw in Garrett's chest. He winced in protest.

"Don't be such a baby," she chided, her voice hitching. "I have to do this."

"Megan…"

His voice was so soft that she could barely hear him. There was too much noise around them; too many people yelling. And there was a rushing sound in her ears, almost engulfing her.

Megan swallowed, afraid to think, afraid to feel anything. "Don't talk," she snapped at him. "Save your strength. You're not going to die, you're not," she insisted tearfully. "Do you hear me, Wichita? I said, you're not allowed to die. You're the good guy. I swear, if you die, I'll never forgive you."

She bent her head over Garrett to see if he was

breathing. Something fluttered weakly against her cheek, but she wasn't sure if it was his breath, or just the air itself.

His eyes were closed.

"You're not allowed to die," she repeated hoarsely. "Do you hear me, you big, dumb jerk? You're supposed to be alive. Don't you die on me." Her heart aching, she whispered against his ear. "I love you, Garrett. Please open your eyes."

Behind her, she heard the wail of sirens getting louder. "The ambulance is here," she told him.

Someone reached to take her arm and help her up, but she slapped the hand away. Rocking, she tightened her arms around Garrett, waiting for the ambulance attendants to arrive. Praying that they weren't too late.

"You can stop playing possum now. They're going to call your bluff."

Her tears fell on his face, but Garrett didn't respond. There was no indication that he had heard anything.

He remained as still as death in her arms.

As still as her heart had become.

Chapter 16

"I'm coming in with you." Her hand held Garrett's tightly as the attendants wheeled him into the emergency room. The steely edge in her voice masked the fact that Megan was as close to hysteria as she had ever been in her life. She'd kept up a steady stream of chatter all the way to the hospital, hoping to rouse him.

He'd never opened his eyes.

The ER physician waved her back to the electronic doors.

"We'll take it from here," he said tersely.

There was no way that she was going to retreat. She needed to be there, in the room, while they worked on Garrett. Needed to be there in case these were the last minutes he had. She wasn't about to let him die alone.

Her eyes met the doctor's as a medical team lifted Garrett onto the examining table. "Not without me."

The chief attendant was rattling off vital signs to him. The doctor nodded as he pulled on a sterile gown. "Lady, you'll do him a whole lot more good keeping out of our way."

Her back to the wall, Megan rested her hand on the swell of the revolver tucked into the waistband of her jeans. Her eyes never left the doctor's face. "I'll keep out of your way in here, not out there."

The doctor threw up his freshly gloved hands, surrendering. But he gave her a last warning. "One word, and I call security."

Megan nodded, her eyes shifting toward Garrett. She was too busy praying and making deals with a higher power to answer.

Staying in the recesses of the room, feeling useless, Megan watched the medical team work through eyes that were hazed with tears. She couldn't think, couldn't focus. All she could do was hold on. And will Garrett to do the same.

Outside, Garrett's friends and the agents who worked with him were all gathering to wait for any news. Kathy and the other girls had been moved to another room at the hotel until morning. All of Velasquez's men had been taken into custody. Velasquez was the only casualty. But all of it could have been happening on Mars for the impact it made on Megan.

Nothing mattered but Garrett.

He'd lost so much blood, she kept thinking. Her

own clothes were soaked with it. How much blood could a man lose and still live?

She was afraid of finding out the answer.

"Here, I think you could use this...."

Megan leaned against the wall outside the first-floor operating room for so long that she no longer knew which of them was holding the other up. She turned her head away from the closed doors, and looked down at the paper cup Oscar was pressing into her hands.

He'd introduced himself to her as Garrett's partner when she'd come out of the ER, following the surgical team as they hurried Garrett into the operating room. His wide, amiable face had been creased with concern, and she'd appreciated it, felt comforted by it.

Megan stared at the dark liquid. "What's this?"

"Coffee. The real stuff. I got it from the shop across the street."

Numb, she nodded and mechanically brought the container to her mouth. The next moment, she couldn't remember if she'd taken a sip or not. With effort, she tried to collect her thoughts. It was past three o'clock in the morning.

It felt as if time had just stopped moving altogether.

"Is Kathy—"

Oscar nodded, anticipating her question. "She's all right," he assured her. "And waiting for you to take her home."

She'd called Kathy's parents just as Garrett was taken into the operating room. Megan remembered barely holding together long enough to assure the couple that their daughter was safe and that she would be on her way home as soon as a few legal details were ironed out.

Operating on automatic pilot, she'd untangled Kathy's involvement in the ring for Garrett's superior when Cassidy had arrived at the hospital. Kathy was free to go, as long as she returned later if her testimony was needed.

She'd deal with that later. Megan looked at her watch. An old-fashioned analog model, the minute hand appeared to have glued itself into place. "What time do you have?"

The smile on Oscar's face was understanding. "Same time you do, Megan. The doctor said it would take a while."

She didn't feel like being patronized. "He didn't say anything about *forever.*" Blowing out a breath, she looked at Oscar. "I'm sorry."

A slight shake of his head told her that she didn't have to bother apologizing. He understood. "Garrett's resilient. I've seen him go through worse."

She looked at the small man and knew he was lying for her benefit. A half smile struggled to her lips. "Thanks."

Caught, Oscar shrugged his wide shoulders.

A few steps away from them, the doors to the operating room opened.

Megan straightened like an arrow, braced for the worst...praying for the best. She was beside the doctor in a heartbeat. "How is he?"

The man tugged his mask down about his neck. He looked exhausted, but pleased. "Luckier than he should be. A quarter of an inch to the right, and you'd be talking to the medical examiner, not me."

"But what's his condition?" Megan pressed.

"Stable. Not that it won't take some time—"

Impatient, Megan cut through the hedging. "He'll live?"

The doctor smiled. "He'll live."

She let out the breath that she seemed to have been holding for the last four hours. Draining the container of coffee by way of celebration, she took one last look toward the operating room. Through the glass, she could see Garrett's gurney being wheeled off. It disappeared through the double doors that led into the recovery room.

Megan crumpled the container and tossed it away. She looked at the surgeon. "Thank you." She'd never meant the words more sincerely than she did at this moment.

With that, she turned on her heel and began to walk away.

"Where are you going?" Oscar called after her.

"To get on with the rest of my life," Megan said as she left.

There was a girl she had to take home—a family to reunite.

Old adages stank, Megan thought moodily, staring at the computer screen in her office. Particularly the one that said "Out of sight, out of mind." The only thing that was apparently going out of mind with Garrett out of sight was *her*.

It had been six weeks—six long weeks—since she'd walked out of the hospital in Reno. Six weeks since she'd brought Kathy Teasdale back to her grateful parents. And four weeks since Wichita had been discharged from the hospital.

She knew exactly when he'd been discharged because up until that time, she'd called the hospital daily—not to talk to him, but to the nurse on call on his floor, in order to get a progress report on his condition. She'd called two, three times a day, until one day she'd been informed that he'd left.

And disappeared from her life.

It was what she wanted, she reminded herself now. To have him gone—completely and irrevocably, so that she could finally get over him.

So why wasn't it happening?

Why was she progressively more irritable with each passing day, instead of progressively more complacent? The fact that he hadn't tried to reach her in the last four weeks shouldn't be bothering her the way it was, shouldn't be stinging her heart. He was only getting on with his life.

The way she should have been with hers.

They were both adults. They both understood one-night stands—or two-night stands, as it were. They'd been just two ships passing in the night, nothing more.

She hurled a paperweight against the wall, breaking off its base.

A minute later, Sam poked his head into her office.

He looked at her a little uncertainly, sort of like Daniel checking out the size and shape of the lions in their den. He glanced at the paperweight on the floor.

"Have we set up a new system of communication nobody told me about? One thud for 'Come in,' two thuds for 'Get lost'?"

Megan gritted her teeth together. If she was ever less in the mood to talk, she couldn't remember when. "I dropped something."

Sam stooped down and picked up the broken paperweight. "All the way across the room?"

Her expression warned him to run for cover if he was smart. "I tripped. It flew out of my hand."

Sam had always liked living on the edge. Crossing to her, he placed the pieces on her desk. "I hate to point this out, Meg, but you're sitting."

"Then don't point it out." Not trusting herself, Megan turned away and glared at her half-empty cup of coffee.

Sam pretended to duck, his hands over his head. "Is that going to 'drop' out of your hands next?"

Afraid that if she started chewing him out for butting in, she wouldn't stop, Megan turned her wrath on something neutral. "Why am I the only one who can make a decent cup of coffee around here?"

"Because you're the only one with access to tar, Megan." Moving the pieces over, he sat down on the edge of her desk and looked at her. "Want to talk about it?"

"The coffee?"

"No," he said pointedly.

Her mouth hardened. There was no way that she

was going to talk to anyone about what she felt. Talking about the hurt would only make it last longer.

"No."

Sam's eyes shifted toward the doorway. "Maybe you'd like to talk to him about it, instead."

"'Him'?"

"Behind you." Sam jerked his thumb toward the doorway.

She turned and saw Garrett standing at the threshold of her office. She was caught off guard as joy and excitement whipped through her like a fierce Kansas twister. Then she was on her feet, hurrying to him. Just as abruptly, she stopped.

This was the man who hadn't picked up a phone to call her in the last four weeks.

Searching for words, determined to hang on to her dignity, she raised her chin—defensive and ready. "You got well."

It was all Garrett could do not to sweep her into his arms, bad shoulder or not. But for now, he followed her lead and kept his hands to himself and his emotions under restraint. "Yeah, I did."

"I'll just go and see if I can find some fresh tar for your coffee," Sam murmured, backing out of the office. Neither seemed to notice him leave.

"How's Kathy?" Garrett asked, testing the waters as the door closed behind Sam.

It took her a minute to recuperate. Her mind had gone completely blank at the sight of him.

"Getting readjusted to the life of a fourteen-year-old. Putting her brief stint in the drug world behind her. No one's bringing any charges against her because of her age and the fact that she was held against her will. The authorities are turning a blind eye to the fact that she supposedly walked into that life willingly. She's not seeing Joe anymore, much to her parents' relief.''

Megan waited a beat. The awkwardness didn't leave. It hung around like an uninvited guest. "So what are you doing here?" she finally asked. "Working on another case?"

Garrett wanted to touch her, to glide his hands along her arms, her face, and assure himself that this time, she wasn't a dream. He stuck his hands in his pockets. "No, I came to look up my sister."

"Your sister?"

"Yeah, the one the nurses told me kept calling every day, asking how I was doing." He watched her eyes, loving the way they darkened. Just the way they did right before they made love. "They all thought it was very unusual that she didn't want to be put through to the phone in my room. I told them that you *were* very unusual." The smile was smug. "I figured it had to be you."

She shrugged. "I was just curious how you were doing."

It went beyond curiosity, and they both knew it. "Oscar said you threatened the ER doctor with a gun."

"I did not." And then the heat left her voice as she gave him details. "I just rested my hand on the gun butt. I can't help what he thought. He wanted to physically eject me from the treatment room."

Oscar had told him about that, too. Along with the fact that most men only dreamed about a woman like

Megan coming into their lives. "People usually wait in the waiting area."

Had he come all this way just to lecture her? Or was he here to gloat because he knew she was in love with him? In either case, she was ready to set him straight. "Like you said, I'm not like most people."

Garrett's eyes swept over her. Was it his imagination, or had she gotten more gorgeous in the last month-and-a-half? "No—that you are not."

Megan felt edgy, and she wanted to wrap this up. To send him on his way before she did something that she was going to regret. "So, you're getting along now? Back to normal?"

Garrett decided to draw the moment out. "Normal's relative. I'm still doing my exercises."

"Exercises?"

"For my shoulder," he explained. The sling had only come off this morning, just before he'd taken the flight out to Orange County. "I checked into a rehab hospital for three weeks. Therapist worked with me every day to get my arm mobile again." And it had paid off. His arm was almost back to the way it'd been before the shooting.

"Three weeks," she repeated. "What did you do for the fourth?"

"Tried to work some things out in my head." The answer was both honest and vague. "Why didn't you come to see me?"

She tried to look indifferent. "Long commute." The flippant tone died on her lips as she looked up at him. "Besides, I thought you'd prefer it this way. Didn't you once say that you liked tying up loose ends and moving on?"

"I did." Unable to resist any longer, he reached up and touched her hair, sifting a strand through his fingers. He watched as a look of desire entered her eyes. "Way I see it, the loose end hasn't been tied up yet."

He was making it hard for her to think. Megan drew her head away. "Meaning?"

"Meaning I need a few answers." His eyes held hers. "No," he amended. "Actually, I just need one."

Was it her, or had the heat suddenly been turned up in her office? "And that is?"

Garrett measured his words. After all was said and done, he didn't know if he was about to tread on solid ground or quicksand. "Well, the answer I need is 'yes.'"

"What's the question?"

His eyes held hers. Didn't she know what was in his heart? Couldn't she see? Was he going to make a fool of himself after he'd climbed out on this limb? "What do you think it is?"

Nerves scrambled through her. Looking away, she began shuffling papers on her desk, wishing the phone would ring. Anything to break this tension. "Look, I've got a lot of work to do. I don't have time for this."

"Make time." Taking hold of her shoulders, he forced Megan to look at him. "Stop running for once in your life, and make time."

Indignation rose in her eyes. He'd found the right button to press.

"I am *not* running."

"Yes, you are," he countered calmly. "You're running just as fast as those gorgeous legs of yours will go."

Who the hell did he think he was, leaving her hanging and out to dry without so much as a word for six weeks, then waltzing in and gloating about it? "We had a couple of nice nights."

She tried to break free, but he wouldn't let her. She was going to hear him out even if he had to sit on her to make her do it. "We had more than that, and you know it. I'm not leaving, Megan, and what's more, you don't want me to."

"Look, Wichita—"

"Garrett," he corrected. "You called me Garrett on the airstrip."

Megan stiffened. He couldn't possibly know that. "You were unconscious—"

He shook his head, his smile curling into her belly. "My eyes were too heavy to keep open, but I wasn't unconscious. I heard you, Megan. I heard you call me Garrett, and I heard what you said afterwards."

He *was* here to gloat. She shrugged him off. "I don't remember what I said."

But he caught hold of her again. The press of his hands was gentle, but firm.

"Yes, you do. You said you loved me. Which works out really well, because I love you." The stunned look on her face encouraged Garrett to continue. "I've tried just as hard to get you out of my mind these last six weeks as you've worked to get me out of yours." It wasn't a guess. He knew her, knew how her mind worked. They were alike, he and Megan. Two halves of the same soul. "I didn't succeed, how about you?"

When she said nothing, he drew her into his arms gingerly, his left arm still hurting.

"Megan, I'm not saying it's going to be easy, but easy's boring, and you're not the type who likes to be bored any more than I am. Now, listen to me." He looked into her eyes, speaking to her heart. "I don't intend to walk out of your life, so you'd better get used to having me around."

It took Megan a moment, but she believed him. Believed that he was here for good. Forever. From where she stood, that had a very, very nice ring to it. "Would you like to ask your question now?"

All or nothing, here it went. He took a deep breath. "Will you marry me?"

She kept her face expressionless. "Is that my only choice? Marriage?"

She was toying with him, right? he thought. He hoped. "Yes."

The sober look melted into a warm smile. Megan wove her arms around Garrett's neck. "Then I guess the answer is 'yes.'"

"Good, because I've got a minister on twenty-four-hour standby." He kissed her then, sealing the bargain. Sealing his life. She tasted better than cool spring water on a scorching hot day. Garrett drank deeply. "God, but I've missed you."

The quick rap on the door interrupted them. "Megan, I've got a new case for you."

Megan and Garrett turned in unison to look at Cade as he entered the room.

The other man stopped abruptly, assessing the situation.

Staying right where she was, in Garrett's arms, Megan shook her head. "I'm afraid that you're going to have to give the case to Sam or take it yourself, Cade. I'm going to be busy.''

He raised a brow. ''Doing what?'' he asked, though he had a hunch he knew what was coming.

She looked up at Garrett. ''Getting married.''

Cade slipped the name and number into his pocket. ''Congratulations, you've come up with the one excuse I'll accept. I'll take care of this one myself.'' First Sam, now Megan. Cade smiled to himself. It was nice to see good people happy, he thought as he closed the door, giving Megan and Garrett privacy.

''He's very accommodating,'' said Garrett.

Megan smiled. ''I taught him everything he knows.''

He lowered his head toward hers. ''Show me.''

''With pleasure,'' Megan replied. She stood up on her toes and met him halfway.

* * * * *

Be sure to look for Cade's story,
HERO IN THE NICK OF TIME, coming only
to Silhouette Intimate Moments in October.

This August 1999, the legend
continues in Jacobsville

DIANA PALMER

LOVE WITH A
LONG, TALL TEXAN

A trio of brand-new short stories featuring
three irresistible Long, Tall Texans

GUY FENTON, LUKE CRAIG
and CHRISTOPHER DEVERELL...

This August 1999, Silhouette brings readers an
extra-special collection for Diana Palmer's legions
of fans. Diana spins three unforgettable stories of
love—Texas-style! Featuring the men you can't get
enough of from the wonderful town of Jacobsville,
this collection is a treasure for all fans!

They grow 'em tall in the saddle in Jacobsville—and
they're the best-looking, sweetest-talking men to be
found in the entire Lone Star state. They are proud,
hardworking men of steel and it will take
the perfect woman to melt their hearts!

Don't miss this collection of original
Long, Tall Texans stories...available in
August 1999 at your favorite retail outlet.

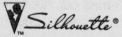

"Fascinating—you'll want to take
this home!"
—**Marie Ferrarella**

"Each page is filled with a brand-new
surprise."
—**Suzanne Brockmann**

"Makes reading a new and joyous
experience all over again."
—**Tara Taylor Quinn**

See what all your favorite authors
are talking about.

Coming October 1999 to a retail store near you.

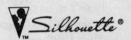

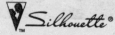

SUMMERS WERE MADE FOR DAYDREAMS AND LOVERS.

AUGUST 1999 JOIN US FOR

Summer DREAMS

BY

DALLAS SCHULZE

See your fantasies come alive and watch the passion sizzle in this three-book compilation by award-winning author Dallas Schulze.

Summer has never been this hot!

Available wherever Harlequin and Silhouette books are sold.

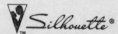